THE TRAIN

THE TRAIN

Tony Jordan

Larry,
All Aboard
Tony Jordan

SPY HILL
PUBLISHING

Library of Congress Control Number: 2015908748
Spy Hill Publishing, Clinton TN

ISBN-13: 9780692456002 (Custom Universal)
ISBN-10: 0692456007

Book design by Nathan Armistead
Printed in the United States of America

To Miss Anne and Tailwagger Jack
without whose encouragement *The Train* would have
remained a short oral parable

ACKNOWLEDGMENTS

WITH THANKS TO RUTH AND Jake for their support and en-couragement throughout the creation of this book, and to Michele and Nathan Armistead for their invaluable assistance throughout the publication process.

CONTENTS

PREFACE

WISE MEN AND GREAT TEACHERS do not tell us what to do. Rather they help us decipher the decision-making process and look within to learn our strengths and overcome our weaknesses. Often by the method of Socrates, they lead us to the realization of action and consequence and, ultimately, to the concept of personal responsibility. Having tutored, they leave us to chart our own paths through the obstacle-strewn field of life.

This is the story of one such teacher and one such student: mentor and pupil; father and son; best friends. Like life, the story is sometimes comical, sometimes heartbreaking, but like a train en route, always moving onward.

THE TRAIN

Summer 1958

CHAPTER 1

THE TRAIN

RAIN SWEPT IN SWELLS ACROSS the metal roof. The noise crescendoed and then abated as each successive swell scoured the metal roof, sweeping it clean of leaves, bird droppings, and branches from the adjacent oak and mimosa trees. On the west side of the house, windows rattled in their frames, assailed by gusts of wind driving the rain horizontally. Visitors from inland cities might have thought themselves caught in a hurricane, but for those of us who lived on the coast, it was just another squall line of summer-afternoon thunderstorms.

Inside, secure against the warm, stinging rain, we sat in the small, neat living room. While we had kept the storm outside, we couldn't stop its darkness from trespassing into the room. So we turned on lamps in the middle of the afternoon.

Hot even with its windows open—now closed and sheltered against the storm—the room felt heavy. The ceiling fan moved the stale, hot, wet air around, not unlike a mixer struggling with bread dough. The noise of the storm outside muted everything else. Even thinking was difficult as I listened to the cacophony of rain and wind against the roof. Waiting for the noise to end, I counted the seconds between swells or the duration of each swell itself.

The house smelled of dampness, Pine-Sol, Johnson Paste Wax, and cherry pipe tobacco. The floors gleamed, reflecting back the lamp light from the polished, darkened pine boards. I sat on the teak bench sofa, its cushions only a little damp from the humidity since they had been recently aired in sunlight on the porch. My father sat in one of the matching teak chairs. He knew the teak pieces in our living room looked more like furnishings that might be found in the solarium of a well-to-do banker; but he also knew that in the high-humidity climate of the Gulf Coast, teak was the most practical wood for furniture, whether you were indoors or out. Our occasional tables were also made from teak. Except for the Boston upright piano against the wall, the room looked more like the cabin of a yacht than the front room of a southern cottage.

"Why so glum?" my father asked.

"Nothing to do," I replied.

To be heard, I raised my voice over the latest swell rolling across the neighborhood. My voice, overmodulated, was unexpectedly too loud as the swell moved on and left only the relative silence of no wind and gently falling rain.

As all fathers would, he answered, "You've plenty to do. We have shelves of books you haven't read. You could oil your ball glove, clean your cleats, practice your piano, or, my gosh, you could clean your room."

None of these things, of course, was what I had in mind about things to do.

"Gee whiz, Dad," I said, "those aren't fun; they're like—work."

"Since when is reading work?" he asked. "I see you with your nose stuck in a book so much that I have to refer to the picture on the piano to remember what your face looks like." He liked the joke and laughed at it himself.

My father was home in the middle of a Thursday afternoon because he was ill. He had just had a heart attack, and he was recovering. He was fifty years old. I was eleven.

"Ha-ha," I responded. "Very funny."

Puns and wordplay were great sources of amusement to my father. A self-educated man, probably brilliant, he worked as a bookkeeper for a number of small businesses owned by a group of semi-prominent Mobilians. He liked the word *Mobilian* because it could refer to someone who lived in Mobile or to the tribe of Indians from whom the town took its name.

"I mean there isn't anything fun to do. Like there is at Donnie Couch's house. Right now he's probably playing with the train set his father built."

"You have a train set," my father countered.

"I have a train set that I have to put together and take apart," I clarified. "It has about five feet of track, and it goes round and round an oval. Donnie has a real train set. It's in the room his grandmother used before she died. It has three trains, tunnels, overpasses, a village with buildings, hills, valleys, and even a river with a bridge over it. It is something!"

My enthusiasm returned as the squall moved off to the northeast.

Spots of sun began to play across the floor as the clouds lost their solidarity. The spots dappled through the branches of the oak tree outside the windows. The tree was at least three hundred years old. The house was probably a hundred and fifty.

The house was in a section of town very near to the Garden District. Members of Mobile society would emphasize, "Ah, yes, that's *very near* the District." Living in "the District" afforded you a certain social status, but because my father was part Choctaw Indian, that status could not be conferred upon us. So it was just as well that we lived near the District and not in it.

"Anyway, it's really neat," I said, continuing my paean to Donnie Couch's train set.

"So what's really neat about it?" my father asked.

"Well…" I described it as it appeared vividly before me. "It has three trains. You can start and stop them all from a control center. Then it has bridges and tunnels. The trains cross over the bridges and go through the tunnels and can stop at the village train station or the water tower. There are couplings you can move to make a train go from one section of track to another. You're in complete control. It's really, really neat."

At eleven, *neat* was the word du jour for expressing satisfaction.

"Yes, I understand it's neat, but where do the trains go?" My father seemed interested.

"Go?" I asked. "What do you mean, where do they go?"

"I mean," he said, "after they go across the bridge, through the tunnel, past the village, and stop at the station or water tower…where do they go?"

"Well…" Here I stopped and thought.

When my father asked a question like this, I had to be careful not to fall into one of his puns or perhaps some moralistic lesson. But thinking back over the exchange to this point, I saw nothing untoward. No trap awaited me.

"Well, they go through the tunnel again and over the bridge," I answered.

"Yes, but where do they go?" he prodded. "Why is it fun? I know you like to play with the controls," he said, encouraging me. "But after the trains go around the track a couple of times, you've done that. Why is it fun to play with the trains at all?"

I thought hard before answering. "Well, you can imagine you're the engineer of the train approaching the tunnel. You have to slow down for the curve ahead. You can imagine you're a passenger waiting in the station or a passenger already on the train, and you're waiting to arrive. It's fun because there are so many people you can be."

"I see," he said. He had been leaning forward, but now he slid back in his chair. He played with his pipe. The doctor wanted him to stop smoking, so he had given up cigarettes for a pipe.

"So it's fun to play with Donnie's train set because you can imagine you're so many different people." He restated my simple explanation.

"That's right." For once my father and I agreed on something.

"But why do you need the trains at all?" he asked.

"I don't understand," I answered. "Why *do* I need the trains at all?"

"That's the question," he affirmed.

"Why wouldn't I need the trains?" I asked again, truly uncertain.

"Well, so far you've told me that the fun is in imagining being this person or that. You don't need the trains to imagine. Do you?"

I thought hard. Was this a trick? The straight line for a joke?

"No, I suppose not," I hazarded a guess. "But it's fun controlling the trains." That was a good answer.

"Yes, but that fun passes quickly," he replied. "You take the trains around the course once, twice, three times. What changes? And where do the trains go?" he asked again.

Once again, I thought hard. Where *did* the trains go?

He interrupted my thought. "Where do *any* trains go?"

"To their destinations," I replied. "They go to their destinations."

"And what is the destination of Donnie's train?" he asked.

Outside, the July sun, having dispersed all but the heartiest of the afternoon cumulonimbus clouds, warmed the asphalt streets so that steam began to appear above the surface. The room was also beginning to heat up as the sun hit the shinier-than-ever tin roof of the house. It was time to think of opening windows.

And with the sun came my realization that Donnie Couch's train went in circles, just like mine. More decorative circles, perhaps, but circles nonetheless. It didn't really go anywhere. If it had a destination, it was only in my mind.

"I see," I said.

"Thought you might," he answered. He put the pipe between his teeth, and I could see him imagining himself a profound thinker. Which, of course, he needed no pipe to be.

CHAPTER 2

A SPECIAL PLACE

"LET'S GO FOR A RIDE!" My father was standing at the door to my bedroom, wearing khaki trousers, a short-sleeved cotton shirt in pale green, and gum-sole canvas deck shoes. His penetrating, dark eyes were hidden behind a pair of tortoiseshell sunglasses. His wavy, jet-black hair was neatly combed to the side, except, of course, for the forelock that defied grooming, continually springing out and curling into the middle of his forehead. He didn't look fifty. He also didn't look like he'd had a heart attack less than a month ago.

Lying across my bed, head hanging off the side, I had an open book on the floor at just the right distance for reading. It was Bullfinch's *Mythology*—a good book, my fallback book, the book I read when I didn't want to start another long book. I was at the place where Theseus was preparing to do battle with the Minotaur. Because I knew how it came out, and because my father was supposed to exercise after his heart attack, I rolled over and hopped up.

"Where to this morning?" I asked.

In late July 1958 in Mobile, early mornings were the only time for outside activities. You could feel the humidity, but the sun hadn't yet begun to lift the dew off the grass or propel the temperature toward the boiling point. I'd already ridden several miles that morning throwing my paper route, but I loved riding my big Roadmaster bike.

"Surprise. Just follow me." He headed for the garage and his new Schwinn Phantom. Well, it wasn't really new. It was just new to him. He had a client who owned a bike shop, and we got good used, reconditioned bikes for a lot less than new bikes cost.

I had gotten over the embarrassment of being seen with my father riding bicycles. When we'd first started riding together, I'd drifted along behind or rode out fast in front. Now we just settled into a leisurely pace, pedaling in time with one another. At age eleven my feet just made firm contact on each pedal at its nadir.

After about a mile or so, I thought I knew where we were going. Looked like we were heading for the port. We always had a good time there. My father knew people who worked the docks, and my uncle Charlie was a harbor pilot. Sometimes we bought fruit off the ships coming in from South America. Sometimes we went aboard the pilot boat for coffee and beignets with Uncle Charlie.

That day, though, we turned short of Government Street. My father led us down a street that got progressively narrower until it ended at a fence. Across the fence was a huge diesel locomotive. The heavy morning air smelled of diesel fuel, exhaust, and ozone. We walked our bikes down a dirt path beside the fence until we came to a gate. My father pushed his bike up to the guard shack and said, "Good morning. We're looking for Mr. Haas."

The guard stepped back in the shack and picked up a telephone. It might have been from the 1930s because the handset appeared to be made of black Bakelite and seemed to weigh three or four pounds. It looked like a dumbbell. Relieved of his responsibility by someone on the phone, the guard pointed down a gravel road toward a set of buildings.

"Mr. Haas is in the switching tower. He's expecting you."

"Thanks," my father said over his shoulder as we pushed our bikes on the gravel.

When we reached the switching tower, we leaned the bikes against a sidewall. We entered through the door under an "Enter" placard. A sticker above a fire alarm handle said, "PULL." My father pointed it out.

"Kind of appropriate in a train yard, don't you think?"

"Appropriate?" I asked.

"Sure, that's what trains do. Pull."

All I could muster was, "Aaarrrgh! That is so weak."

By that time we had climbed the stairs. I watched my father closely for any signs of distress, like shortness of breath, but he seemed OK. At the top of the stairs, we came out into a modest-sized room. It was completely surrounded by large plate-glass windows. Although it was only three stories high, it seemed as if I could see forever. To the east I could see the bay; north was town. To the south I could see the control tower at

Brookley Air Force Base and the planes using its runway. But mostly I could see the entire marshaling yard for the trains that serviced both Brookley and the Mobile docks.

"Trains from Mobile go to destinations all over the United States," stated Mr. Haas. My father played poker with him. He lived in our neighborhood. I went to school with his daughter, Linda. He was the shift manager for the yard.

"All over the United States," he repeated, as if it needed emphasis.

I was still awestruck at the view. When you lived in the flatlands along the Gulf Coast, a view from a height was a real treat. I turned around in a circle, trying to take it all in. I couldn't.

"And planes from Brookley Field fly all over the world, just like ships from the port sail all over the world," my father added. He still called Brookley by its World War II Army Air Corps designation. He'd never really accepted a separate air force.

My father was proud of Mobile. He was a native, and his family had been there since 1804, when his great-whatever grandfather arrived from South Carolina. In 1812 that grandfather purchased twenty thousand acres in the newly expanded Mississippi Territory. The land was just to the north of Mobile, so over the generations, many members of the family moved to the city. They became part of its history.

So why, then, was he an orphan? Why, when his father died, had he been placed in a Roman Catholic orphanage for boys? Why had he remained there for eleven years? The answer was simple. His mother was a Choctaw Indian. No child with white blood could be raised by an Indian. Better that the Jesuits did it. But why hadn't one of his relatives taken him in? That was what my father always wanted to know. Why?

"All over the world," my father continued. "Think about it. That ship over there could be leaving for Japan. Those airplanes could be on their way to Iran or India." He gestured as he spoke, first to the port and then off toward the airbase.

It was a lot to take in. At eleven, never having been farther away from home than central Mississippi and New Orleans, I found it difficult even to imagine such travels. It had been only the day before that my father had led me to conclude that my imagination could take me anywhere; now he was showing me the real world of going anywhere. Electric train sets, no matter how extravagant, could not convey the idea of traveling the world. That was why my father had asked, "But where do the trains go?" when I kept telling him how neat having a large train set would be.

"That train over there is a combination," said Mr. Haas, pointing to a long train that was being formed up on a track across the yard. "Do you know what a combination is?" he asked me.

"Uh, let's see. Combination? Of course. It's when you have boxcars, passenger cars, coal cars, and oil cars all in the same train," I answered.

"Well, you almost have it." he said. "No oil or coal cars are on a combination. Just freight and passenger cars. Oil, coal, and gas cars contain what is considered hazardous material, so we never combine them with passenger cars."

He put his hand on the small of my back. He was guiding me to the large, slanted console, which had a layout of the entire train yard superimposed on it. There were small lights all over. Some were red; others were green and yellow. Laid out along the depiction of the tracks, there were numerous black handles.

"OK, we have a sleeper car coming up from the lower yard to join the combination. It is on track five, and the combo is forming up on track seven. We need to move it two tracks. To do that we have to use a junction switch, first from track five to six and then from six to seven." He looked out at the yard. A switch engine was moving the sleeper car from the south to the north on track five. He motioned to one of the black handles.

"Turn this so the green light above it comes on."

I reached out and turned the handle. It went only from a down position to a sideways position. The green light came on.

"That's five to six," he said. He looked out at the tracks. "Now this one." He pointed to a handle above the last and slightly to the left.

I turned the handle. Again a green light came on.

"That's six to seven. Now we watch for the sleeper and switch engine to clear each switch, and we reset them. That's how we move cars around the yard."

I couldn't help thinking that it must get boring, although the thought of train cars crashing together or coming off the tracks nagged at the back of my brain. I didn't think I would want the responsibility. I remembered too many mistakes just trying to switch trains around on Donnie Couch's train set.

Man! I thought. If I had derailed a real diesel locomotive, I'd have been amazed if a crew could have gotten it upright again. At Donnie's we just stood on a stool, leaned over the table, and picked it up with our hand.

We thanked Mr. Haas, reclaimed our bikes, and pedaled toward the station. It was cooler inside the station with all the ceiling fans and open doors. We bought RC Colas and boiled peanuts from the concession-cum-book stand and lunch counter. Taking them out to the platform, we sat on a bench in the shade. There was a passenger train boarding. We watched the passengers and porters going up and down, getting in and out of the cars.

"That one's going all the way to Chicago." My father pointed to the placard next to the door of a car. The next car down had "St. Louis" on its placard.

"How long to Chicago?" I asked.

"Better part of a day and a half, I imagine," he answered.

"You imagine or you know?" I asked, tongue in cheek. (Actually my tongue *was* in my cheek. I'd gotten a peanut caught between my gum and the side of my mouth.)

"Well, we can always go back inside and look at the board." He nodded his head toward the lobby, where the departures and arrivals board loomed above the waiting area.

"But speaking of imagining," he continued, "we can sit right here on this bench and take the train to St. Louis or Chicago—or anywhere, for that matter. You know, after a while even those plush-looking seats in the passenger cars will get as hard as this bench. We'll have to get up and move around. On some trains there's an observation car, and there's always the dining car, but we just go there at the times we've signed up for our meals. Of course there's always the sway." Here he started to move a little to his left and then his right, then left, then right. "And some roads are bumpy as well." He added a little up and down to his left and right. "There's the sound too." He clicked his teeth.

So there was my father up and downing, left and righting, clicking his teeth. He looked at me. "Come on, get on the train."

Slowly I matched his sway, then his up and down. I didn't try clicking.

Then he pointed to one side. "Look at all those Jersey cows. Must be a dairy."

I looked to where he was pointing. There was a porter with a large hand truck and several suitcases. He was staring.

"Coming to a bridge…Here we go across the Mississippi." At this point my father added more vertical to his upping and downing.

I stopped, embarrassed by the stare of the porter. My father kept on. I reached up and tugged on his sleeve.

"Dad, people are staring," I whispered somewhat too loudly. He stopped, took a long swig from his still cool RC, and then looked down at me. He was grinning from ear to ear.

"Son, they're just staring because they want to go with us." He turned to the porter. "Plenty of room here on this bench! We're going to Chicago." He grinned at the porter, who grinned back and then put his shoulder to the hand truck.

My father turned back to me and said, "Being stared at isn't necessarily a bad thing. When people stare at you, just smile at them and then invite them in on whatever you're doing. They'll want to join, but most times they won't." Yet another profundity from my father, I thought.

"How do you know all this stuff?" I asked as he bounced and swayed momentarily, then stopped again.

"Experience. I know because I've tried other ways, and they didn't work as well as this or that. Yep, just trial and error. If something doesn't work, try something else. You, on the other hand, get the benefit of my experience. For example, imagining can be fun and productive. If you imagine how you're going to do something before you do it, you can anticipate problems and work them out beforehand. That's called practicing. Just like playing the clarinet."

Did I mention my father was also a really good musician?

"Now, imagining for fun is great, but it's always more fun if someone else is imagining with you." His voice had dropped, and the last part came out almost wistfully.

We headed back through the lobby for our bicycles. I thought about what he'd said. *Experience* meant he had lots of experience imagining. But he seemed so much of a doer. He was almost never still—well, more since he'd had the heart attack, but before that he was almost never still. When had he had time to imagine? When had he learned all these things?

I followed, but we didn't head home. Instead we stopped at the library. Mobile had a fine library, and it had air conditioning. The two-story, large-windowed, white building looked like libraries should look, distinguished and fitting of its place on Government Street, surrounded by three-hundred-year-old oak trees and the Church Street Cemetery.

Inside it was cool and much drier. I hated the thought of going out again, but still, I didn't like air conditioning either. I always felt so cold inside, and then when I went out again, the heat felt much worse because the difference between the inside and outside temperatures was so much greater with air conditioning.

My father took me to the reference section, to a shelf filled with books about states and cities. He pulled a book on Chicago from the shelf and opened it to a group of pictures in the middle.

"OK, what do we want to see in Chicago?" he whispered, his head close to mine. "Over here," he instructed. He took me around the shelves to a small desk set against the wall, near a window that looked out to the rear of the building, over the graves of the cemetery. It was a nice spot and very out of the way of the rest of the activity of the library.

"This is my favorite spot," he said as he sat in the chair at the writing desk. I leaned over his shoulder. We looked at the pictures in the book. Lake Michigan, the Loop, State Street, the museums, the tall buildings. Some of the photos had been taken from an airplane. The city was so big. My father and I spent almost half an hour looking through the book, discussing, in conspiratorial voices, where we wanted to go when our train reached Chicago.

After he put the book back on the shelf, we left the library and took up our bikes for the ride home. It wasn't far, but the heat had gotten worse, and the humidity made it feel like we were riding through very wet Kleenex. I watched my father closely. We were too far from a hospital for a quick response. As we rode along, I continually looked for places that had telephones, so I could call for help if needed.

We made it home, although I could tell the ride in the heat and humidity had taken the energy out of my father. I suggested he sit in the living room and let me bring him something cool to drink.

While opening the ice trays, I wondered how my father knew of the small desk and how and when it had become his favorite place. I wondered how he'd gotten so much experience imagining.

I squeezed the lemons, added the sugar, stirred the mixture, and took my father a pitcher of cold lemonade. As I passed through the dining room, my eye caught my father's high school graduation picture on the wall in the hallway. It had been taken in 1926 in front of the orphanage. There were two rows of students. In the first row, the students were kneeling. In the second row, they were standing. My father was in the second row at the end, standing away from the others, as if he didn't quite belong. I understood more about imagining and the library.

December 1958

CHAPTER 3

I Shall Be First
Captain

"How do you do, sir? I am proud to meet you." No, that wouldn't do. "How do you do, General?" I paused. "Dad, do you call a general of the armies *general* or *general of the armies?*"

"I think *general* works for all the general officer grades." My dad had been in the army briefly before being medically discharged. Since he knew everything else, I assumed he would know how to address Gen. Douglas MacArthur.

I had imagined myself meeting General MacArthur—let's see, maybe five thousand times. Each time I shook the General's hand as he emerged from the doors of the Waldorf-Astoria. He asked me how I was doing and whether I would go to West Point. Each time I told him I was very well and, indeed, would go to West Point and be first captain. He then congratulated me on my appearance and demeanor, and, before he entered his waiting car, he touched the brim of his cap in salute. I snapped to attention and returned the acknowledgment.

Each time I imagined it, the conversation got just a bit longer. The exchange became just a tad more mature. This wasn't a hero speaking to a child; it was a general speaking to a subordinate whom he held in high regard.

My father said General MacArthur was the greatest general since Robert E. Lee. I believed him. To be placed in the same pantheon as Lee was high praise indeed. In December 1958, in Mobile, Alabama, the war was hardly over—and I don't mean World War II. My father, although raised in an orphanage because his mother was a Choctaw Indian, was proud of his family's heritage. He was proud that his family fought the English in the revolution, the Mexicans in 1848, the Spanish in Cuba, the Germans in the First and Second World Wars, and the Koreans and Chinese in Korea. We were just a fighting family, I guess. I mean, my cousins and I surely fought a lot. It must have been in our blood, as my grandmother said.

"I think you're going to melt in that coat and sweater," said my mother, who was sitting on the bench-like sofa we had in our living room. She was referring to the heavy wool pea jacket and the submariner's turtleneck sweater I was trying on for the four- or five-hundredth time. We had gotten them at a used clothing store where many seamen sold their clothes when they were hard up for cash. My mother had unstitched the lining, boiled the wool jacket down until it fit me, and then cut and tacked a much-reduced lining back into the coat. We could have just bought something new, but that would have offended my parents' Depression-era sense of value.

I was worried that trying to meet General MacArthur while wearing something so navy-like might cause him to pass me by.

"Dad, are you sure General MacArthur won't ignore me if I'm wearing this navy-blue jacket? After all, Army hates Navy." This was about the tenth time I'd sought reassurance on this matter.

"Son, I guarantee you have the same chance of meeting General MacArthur wearing that pea coat as if you were wearing the uniform of a West Point first captain."

"Gee, Dad, do you think so?" In my enthusiasm I missed the obvious.

My mother smiled at my father, who grinned back. I saw them but still didn't get it. OK, I didn't get it because I didn't want to get it.

I didn't know just how I knew General MacArthur lived in the Waldorf-Astoria, or, as I had been told New Yorkers said, the Waldorf. I just did. I'd wanted to meet him forever—well, as long as forever can be when you're a precocious eleven-year-old. At the time I hadn't been sure what *precocious* meant. I couldn't look it up in the dictionary because I couldn't spell it, but that was what my father said I was all the time—precocious. I thought I just might march up to my dad and ask him how to spell *precocious*. Then again, I might not. It might not be something I wanted to know. After all, my dad was my best friend, and I didn't want to know if he thought I was too big for my britches or something like that.

My dad's heart attack had been last June. He was much better a month later and had gone back to work full time. He was a bookkeeper. Not just your everyday counting-numbers bookkeeper. He was the bookkeeper for a group of up-and-coming Mobile businessmen who were gobbling up businesses like my dog ate his dinner. They owned all the taxicab companies, all the really good restaurants, two of the hotels, a lot of garages where you got your car fixed, a savings and loan association, lots of rental properties, and some things I wasn't supposed to know about. Even knowing about those things, I didn't mention them. People might have thought I really didn't know about them, but I did. For example, there were some nightclubs, roadhouses, and, well, other things I wasn't supposed to understand until I was older. They also had a lot of city contracts for things like repairing the city buses and school buses. Things like that.

I sometimes went with my father when he made his rounds of the businesses, and, although he might have thought I couldn't overhear him talking with the other men, I had the hearing of a good dog. Not the ears, mind you, just the hearing.

Since going back to work, my father had been asked to go to New York City. He was going with some of his bosses to meet some people about investing money in a project in Mobile. It was a secret, but I knew they were going to talk about opening three new marinas. One on Dog River, one on Fowl River, and one on Dauphin Island. The secret wasn't the marinas. It was that Yankee money would be backing the effort. Yankee money was a sin in Mobile. But it was only a sin, my father said, because the local bankers wanted to control everything. He didn't think that was right, and neither did his bosses, who had gotten tired of having to pay off the local bankers with larger percentages of their profits.

So we were going to New York. My only knowledge of New York had come from the reference section in the library, where I'd spent the better part of the previous two weeks. I'd also seen most of the Bowery Boys movies, but I thought they might have been made in Hollywood and not New York. Besides, people didn't really talk like that, did they? That would have been a good question for my dad. He'd been to New York several times. He'd know if the people there were really that hard to understand.

I found him in the living room. He was sitting in a chair facing the fireplace. It was one of the few days in the year when we could use the fireplace. It was forty-five degrees outside. We were having a cold spell. By Christmas it would be up in the sixties again. Since we didn't have a lot of fires, we burned pinewood and oak. We weren't too concerned with the creosote buildup.

Coming up behind my father, I saw his hands moving. He was imagining. I thought he was imagining his meeting with the potential investors. He called it visualizing. I moved to the side and watched from the edge of the dining room arch.

His eyes were closed. He sat upright; his hand moved as he picked up invisible pieces of paper and showed them to the investor. He stopped. Then his hands moved differently. He didn't like the last effort. He changed and seemed to find the new gestures more pleasing. He moved on. I studied him closely. I had learned from him how to control my emotions better and how to anticipate what otherwise might have been unexpected movements on the parts of others. I saw him shift his body weight. He had become the potential client responding. He was thinking like the other person, imagining his responses, his body movements, his words. By the time he went into the meeting, he would have imagined and responded to all the potential bad and good things that could happen.

I didn't interrupt him. I returned to my room, sat in my reading chair, and imagined the Chrysler Building's silver top, the view from the Empire State Building, the Statute of Liberty, and, of course, my meeting with General MacArthur. I intended to stand in front of the Waldorf and wait until he left or arrived. My father said our hotel was very near the Waldorf, and he didn't mind if I waited on the General while he attended his meetings. I was sure the General must be a busy man and would be coming and going from his suite constantly.

"Yes, sir, I shall attend West Point and become first captain." He would be pleased to hear that, I was sure.

My mind took me once more through the trip. We would leave from the Mobile station on Christmas afternoon. The train would go north through the swamplands en route to Montgomery, east across the plains to Atlanta, and then northeast over the Blue Ridge Mountains to Washington, DC. In Washington we would change trains on the morning of December 27 and travel up the Eastern Seaboard to New York City. We would arrive at Pennsylvania Station—Penn Station to the natives—just before noon on the twenty-seventh. Then we would take a taxi to our hotel just off Fifth Avenue.

Christmas morning was a whirlwind of activity. We had been going constantly for two days. Midnight Mass was followed by our traditional late night/early morning breakfast at the Café Royale. Some sleep, beignets, and café au lait, then presents. My parents gave me a Japanese thirty-five-millimeter camera. Every moment was part of an ever-tightening spiral drawing us toward the eventual departure.

Everybody went to the station. My aunt and uncle came. Aunt Belle presented us with a basket containing several pimento-cheese and bologna sandwiches. The cheese sandwich was my favorite, the bologna my father's. There were also several bottles of RC Cola and a cut-up pecan pie. Uncle Charlie wrapped a white wool scarf around my neck. "Stay warm!" he said. I didn't know how I was supposed to wear a scarf and a turtleneck at the same time.

My mother cried, but then she always cried whenever my dad left town. My cousins were too young to care. We just had to keep watching them so they didn't wander off the platform and under the trains.

We found the railcar we were in, and our family climbed the steps to see our compartment. Not everyone could fit inside it. It was funny—a compartment looked so much bigger in the movies. I had imagined it bigger. *Oh, well,* I thought. In the future when I imagined a train compartment, I would get it right.

The conductor really did call, "All aboard!" My dad and I sat facing one another across the narrow compartment. The seats were harder than I'd expected. We waved to everyone as the train jerked away from the platform.

My father had been right the previous summer when he had been imitating the motion of a train. It did jerk up and down while swaying left and right. We waved until we were out of sight and then a little more. It was not as quiet as I had imagined. The train's whistle shrieked near the first crossing, as the train rocked from side to side, our progress slower than I could ride my bike. I caught glimpses of buildings I knew, streets where I rode my bike, houses on my paper route. I thought of poor Uncle Charlie. He was going to have to supervise Donnie Couch throwing my paper route until I returned.

We neared the edge of town, crossing onto the elevated track that ran through the swamps of the Mobile and Alabama Rivers. We picked up speed, and the rocking became a regular left, right, left, right. The wheels did click in rhythm on the rails. My father sat back. I sat back as well. He smiled. I smiled back.

"It's going to be a great experience," he said. His enthusiasm was obvious.

"It already has been," I responded. My eyes focused on the horizon, my face reflected on the window in the early evening twilight. "Yes, sir, I shall go to West Point and become first captain."

CHAPTER 4

A Real First Captain and More

I LOOKED AT MY WATCH. It was ten past four. The light had already gone from what little sky could be seen from the man-made canyons of New York City. The portico of the Waldorf-Astoria was brightly lit. My feet were cold. The pavement was cold, and it seeped through the soles of my shoes. My nose was cold and runny. My fingers were stiff but still a little warm in the gloves Uncle Charlie had given me. Besides, I was spending so much time wiping my nose that my fingers didn't have a chance to get too cold. Still, December 30, 1958, was finishing up as one of the coldest days of my eleven years.

I had stood at the Waldorf most of the day and the day before as well but had not seen General MacArthur. The day before, when I'd first come, I'd offered to bribe Michael, the doorman, with one of the remaining pimento-cheese sandwiches Aunt Belle had prepared for our trip. I had it in my pocket. It was only a little stale. The doorman laughed and, after a bit, agreed that if the General was going out, he would tell me when they called down for his car. This day, unfortunately, when I arrived just before noon, the doorman told me the General had already gone out, not a half hour before. Well, at least I knew the General was out. He had to return. So I was standing where the doorman assured me I would be out of trouble's way. I continued to wait.

I occasionally talked to some of the bellmen as they carried luggage in and out of the hotel. There was Tony from Jersey and Arnold from "Da Bronx." Arnold really talked like one of the Bowery Boys. Yet in my young, inexperienced mind, the Bronx was a bit removed from the Bowery. I planned to test this theory the next morning. I would take the subway to the Bowery, and I would determine if the Bowery Boys might really have been from the Bronx or if they talked funny in the Bowery as well. Arnold was happy being a bellman, but Tony wanted to be called Anthony because he thought he could move up faster if his name was a little more formal. He was trying to talk the bell captain into giving him a new nametag. Only when Tony and Arnold said "Anthony," it seemed to come out more like "Ant-ny." I didn't think that was much of a formal name, but then I was not from New York.

The bell crew didn't mind me because I explained that while I had come to New York City with my father on business, my real reason was to meet General of the Army Douglas MacArthur. I explained how General MacArthur was one of the greatest generals in the history of the country. They pretty much agreed with me, and besides, they had come to think of me as a minor celebrity in my own right. I had mentioned that on Sunday, after arriving on Saturday, my father and I had gone to see the New York Giants play the Baltimore Colts in the world championship football game. It had been a surprise for both of us. When we'd arrived at the hotel, the tickets had been waiting. They were a gift from the potential business client my father would be meeting.

So on Sunday my father and I had stood in Yankee Stadium. Nobody sat, not from the time everyone rose for the national anthem. The game was too exciting. And besides, being short, I had to stand just to see. It was the first championship ever to go to overtime.

We rooted for the Giants, partly because we thought it proper to root for the home team since we were, after all, in New York, and I had never even been to Baltimore. My father had, but he said it didn't really count because it was a business trip. But mostly we rooted for the Giants because they had Charlie Conerly as quarterback. He was from Mississippi, and he had served valiantly as a marine in the war before returning to Ole Miss. The Colts' quarterback, Johnny Unitas, was from Pittsburgh, Pennsylvania. We didn't begrudge Mr. Unitas his chance at glory and, since there were no professional football teams in the South, we recognized that Baltimore (and the Washington Redskins) came the closest to being home teams for whom we southern boys and dads might cheer. Still, my father and I thought we should cheer for someone who was from a little closer to home than Baltimore or Pittsburgh.

By the time Baltimore's Alan Ameche went over right tackle for the game-winning touchdown, both my father and I were too cold to care. Later, our hotel suite seemed like an oven, and we felt like frozen dinners. After thawing out we were too tired for anything but sandwiches from Aunt Belle's basket and bed.

Still the bell crew accorded me minor hero status, for tickets to the "Greatest Game Ever Played," as the newspapers were calling it, had been impossible to come by. Many guests at the Waldorf had been most disappointed when the concierge could not supply them. "Isn't this the Waldorf? I stayed here specifically because I was told the Waldorf could get tickets for anything." One of the guests had made this pronouncement somewhat piercingly on Saturday. Or so Tony told me.

I checked my watch again. It was a Waltham wristwatch my grandfather had given me two years before. It kept good time if I remembered to wind it. I didn't really have to look at the watch, though, because there was a ship's clock just behind the bell captain's desk, and it too read fifteen minutes after four. My father and I had agreed to meet in front of the Waldorf at four thirty. There were only fifteen minutes left. Getting warm wouldn't be much of a consolation prize if I didn't get to meet General McArthur, I thought, but it would be better than not seeing the General and staying cold. I simply could not imagine how people in the North lived there in the winter.

My camera was heavy on my neck. I had practiced holding it up, snapping a photo, and winding the winding knob without taking my eye from the viewfinder. I had several pictures of the doorman and the bell captain as well as Tony and Arnold.

I hoped the bright lights of the Waldorf entrance would make up for not having a flash. The camera hadn't come with one.

At four twenty-five a large, black Cadillac drew to the curb. The doorman gave me the high sign as he moved to open the rear passenger-side door. I looked for the General, but there was only an old man in a dark wool coat in the car. He exited the car slowly, a cane in his right hand. As he turned slightly to avoid the door edge, he came into profile, and his aquiline nose was unmistakable. He was General of the Army Douglas MacArthur. The General straightened; he placed one of those funny hats—either a humbug or a hamburger, I believed—on his head. He spoke to the doorman. "Well, Mick, how's the family?"

"Just fine, General," Mick said. "Thank you for asking. Uh, General, you have an admirer who has waited most of yesterday and today to get a picture." He nodded in my direction. Good ole Mick!

This is it! I thought. The General looked at me. I was petrified. I neither snapped to attention nor extended my hand.

He asked, "And what is your name, young man?"

Name! *Name?* That was not part of my rehearsed role. I had not anticipated the General would ask my name.

He switched his cane to his left hand and proffered his right. It was large. Much larger than mine. They say training will save you when an emergency occurs. Indeed, it did. My training as a young southern gentleman kicked in, and I took his hand in mine. I grasped it firmly but not too firmly. I pumped it once and withdrew my hand.

I managed to say, "Pleased to meet you, sir." And then that training, with its ten years of repetition, kicked in again. "My name is Jack...Jack Jourdain. I'm from Mobile, Alabama."

"And I am pleased to meet you, Jack. Does that camera work?"

Camera? What camera? My mind sought answers. Oh, yes, the one hanging from my neck.

"Yes, sir, it works."

"Well then, perhaps Mick can take a picture of us. Would you like that?"

We southern boys might stagger from the first blow, physical or metaphysical, but our southern mothers didn't raise wimps. I had recovered.

"Absolutely, sir," I replied. I was my father's son and my grandfather's grandson.

I handed Mick the camera and said, "General, my great-grandfather had the honor to be at Chattanooga when your father won the Medal of Honor."

"Did he now? What was his regiment?"

"The Forty-First Alabama, sir. He was a lieutenant. He was eighteen years old."

"And my father was nineteen. That seems fitting. And you, young Jack. Will you be a soldier?"

"It is my intention, sir, to go to West Point. I shall try to become first captain, as you were." We were standing next to one another; the General had his right hand on my left shoulder. In his left hand he held his cane loosely. He did not use it to steady himself.

A flash went off. My camera didn't have a flash. My eyes had little balls of light traveling about them. The balls of light moved to the center of wherever I tried to look. The hand was off my shoulder, and I felt my right hand being shaken again. There was another flash.

"Well, Jack, I wish you the greatest of luck in your endeavors."

"Thank you, sir." I snapped to attention and saluted.

He raised his cane, now back in his right hand, to the brim of his humbug—or was it hamburger?—hat. Mick opened one of the side doors, and the General strode through.

I stood, hand still in salute, until he disappeared. *Ready, two.* I thought of the military command and dropped my hand to my side.

A man in a suit with a press camera handed me a slip of paper. "The photographs will be ready in two hours. You can pick them up at the concierge desk," he said. I looked at Mick. He was smiling as if he'd just won the Derby lottery.

"I thought the hotel might like to have a picture of the General's fan club," he said. "After all, this is the Waldorf." His uniform buttons shone brightly in the lights of the portico. He rushed to help a lady exit the hotel. She needed a cab, so he went to the curb and blew his whistle. From down the street, a yellow cab appeared. He opened the door for the lady. She handed him a dollar bill. He touched the brim of his cap and returned. He was still smiling.

The photographs had caused a small crowd to form on either side of the portico. I heard people speaking.

"Who is he?"

"I don't know, who do you think he is?"

"Who was that who went through the door?"

From the edge of this small crowd, my father stepped into the lights of the portico. "So, you did get to meet the General."

There were too few words available to an eleven-year-old to explain my feelings. My father shook Mick's hand and introduced himself. Mick handed him my camera. Tony walked by with some luggage on a cart and said hello. I felt my father's hand on my shoulder guiding me away from the bright lights.

"The pictures!" I blurted out.

"Won't be ready until later. They have your name. I gave it to Mick. They'll hold them for us. Let's eat early. There's a nice small restaurant a few blocks over."

Seated at the table, I still hadn't said more than, "Hot chocolate, please," and, "I prefer blue cheese dressing, if you have it."

My father had been quiet as well. He sipped the Manhattan he'd ordered.

"Well, Jack," he said. He didn't call me *boy* or *son*, as he normally did. "Well, Jack, you did it. But then I'm not really surprised. Your life has always had those special brief, charm-like episodes. And I have no reason to believe it will not continue to be so."

The hot chocolate had warmed me to the point I began to revive. I nudged myself away from imagining the possibilities of the future and back into the real world.

"Dad, he wished me luck in my endeavors. General MacArthur wished me not just luck but the greatest of luck. He said, 'Jack, I wish you the greatest of luck in your endeavors.' The greatest of luck!"

My father looked over his glass at me. We locked eyes, his deep black eyes into my still-forming green ones.

"Yes, he did, Jack. He wished you luck. And you know the definition of luck, don't you? We've talked about it scores of times."

"Yes, sir. Luck is the intersection of preparation and opportunity."

"Yes, it is, Jack. Remember that. And as the General said, the greatest of luck in your endeavors."

December 1961

CHAPTER 5

VICTORY

THE SMALL FINGER ON MY right hand was bigger than a brat-wurst. It was broken or, at the very least, grossly dislocated. My forearm, purple by the end of the first quarter, was now a greenish black. My head pounded, and my nose bled from the cut across its bridge, but I felt great. I had never felt so good before. This was what moral vindication felt like. Moral vindi-cation and physical domination.

The crowd poured onto the field like water through down-spouts in a thunderstorm. Everyone was patting me on the back and slapping me on the shoulder pads. Many grabbed at my hand to shake it. *It hurt!* I stuck my right hand inside my helmet and offered my left to those who were grabbing. At five foot ten even in my cleats, I couldn't see over the people, but I knew where he was sitting. I made my way toward the stands at the forty-yard line. I saw my mother standing on the bleacher seat, waving the red scarf above her head. She was try-ing to attract my attention. I jogged toward her. People were in my way, but I didn't stop or slow. I wasn't interested in their congratulations. I didn't care if they received vicarious pleasure from speaking to or touching the game's most valuable player. I wanted only to see my father.

He sat on the first row of the bleachers. He wore a turtle-neck, now so big for his frame that he appeared to be wearing someone else's clothes. It wasn't fair, first a heart attack and now leukemia. Not fair at all. But he was laughing. Not smiling—laughing. The illness had not taken the light from his eyes. I found the stairs to the stands and climbed them, surging against the current of spectators spilling onto the field. My uniformed presence loomed over him as I reached the seats. My bright-red jersey, in the glare of the stadium lights, did not hide the blood that was accentuated where it had saturated the white number thirty-three. The white pants also showed rust-colored spots of blood. I knelt in front of him. He took up my hand and looked at the finger and the forearm.

"They don't hurt," I assured him.

"Not now they don't, but they will." His voice was weak but clear.

"No, sir," I was resolute in my defiance. "They will not hurt, I assure you."

He smiled, took my head in his hands, and pulled me close. He kissed my forehead. Then, looking into my eyes, he said, "Go accept your wreath of laurel, but remember that all glory is fleeting, and that you are still a mortal." He counseled me as if I were a Roman general returning victorious from the boundaries of the empire.

But for the first time in my memory, he was wrong, for that night I was not mortal. I was a demigod. I had swept my opponents from the field both physically and metaphorically. I did not command Olympus, but for forty-eight minutes that night I had stood atop the crowned field at Ladd Memorial Stadium, where I had commanded my outmanned troops, as Leonidas had his Spartans. And like the Spartans, we had turned back the superior force time after time until time ended. My opponents had not passed. (Well, actually, they had passed more than a few times, but they completed only the very short ones.)

I could have kept my reverie going a lot longer, but I had to find the Catholics' coach. I had missed him on the field. I had to deliver the coup de grace. The shot to the head, if you will. He deserved it.

From the stands I looked down into the field. He was heading for the exit to my left.

"Excuse me, Dad," I said, smiling at my mother as I moved off as quickly as I could while wearing steel-tipped cleats and walking on concrete. Reaching the field, I saw a lane open next to the wall of the stands. I sprinted to my left. I pushed through the wall of reporters, fans, and players around Coach Madinger. At six foot three, he was much taller than I was. He kept saying, "No comment, no comment." I was behind him and grabbed him lightly by the shoulder. He turned. I extended my left hand.

Caught by surprise, and surrounded by newspaper and TV reporters, he had no option. First he reached with his right, then, realizing I had my left hand out, he changed and took my hand with his left. He had a firm grip and, I thought, would crush my hand given the opportunity. I didn't give him the chance. I squeezed back. I knew what I wanted to say. I had visualized myself saying it a thousand times over the last month. No, not a thousand; maybe ten thousand. It was there in my head. I would smile triumphantly and speak the words loudly enough so the reporters and nearby players could hear: "Who do you think Notre Dame would rather have tonight? Me or you?"

But I did not. As much as this man deserved to be embarrassed publicly, I would not do it. Instead I looked him in the eyes, pumped his hand once, let go, spun on my heel, and walked off toward the center of the field. He was vanquished. I had ended the affair on my terms. Although I was not satisfied, I was reconciled that justice would be done. He couldn't answer "no comment" forever.

My father had been right; they hurt. Mostly it was the finger, broken just above the knuckle. My arm throbbed from the swelling, but it looked worse than it was. It had taken on the shiny green-and-dark-purple hue of maggot-infested meat. I refused to wear a sling. Instead I kept my hand in the pocket of my blazer. I did not take it out because I was sure it looked infected. I had a small Band-Aid across the bridge of my nose. The slightest tinge of purple was revealed from under the edges of the Band-Aid, but, if anything, it gave me the look of a devil-may-care rascal. My grandfather always called me a rascal when he thought I was getting away with something. So yes, perhaps I was at times a rascal.

The party was nice. In our small house, thirty people created a real crush. We were in the living room mostly, but several people still stood round the table in the dining room. They were chowing down on the shrimp, crab claws, crayfish cakes, and other Gulf Coast delicacies the Café Royale had brought over for the party. The manager was in the kitchen with two of his best cooks. He would leave shortly so as not to miss a major business night at the café, but he was a close friend of my father's and had insisted on doing this. I was glad. It was a wonderful party. My aunts and uncles were there. Although I had no blood relation with most of them, they were still my aunts and uncles. Some of them did not have children and treated me as a son. Some even called me *son* when we spoke privately. At fourteen I was a lucky young man.

The car would come at six to take me, my mother, and my aunt Betty to the awards banquet. My uncle Gale had arranged it. He owned a group of auto garages along the Gulf Coast. He was one of my father's oldest friends. Unlike my father, who was only a half-breed, my uncle Gale was a full-blood Choctaw. My father and Uncle Gale would not attend the banquet. My father was using his illness as an excuse, but I knew he was not going because the dinner was at an all-white country club. It was a club that would not have him as a member, so he saw no reason to go as a guest. I understood. I doubted they would have me as a member when I was grown. I'm a quarter Choctaw.

The mayor and the archbishop would be at the banquet. Henri, the manager of the Café Royale, knew the people catering the dinner, and they would tell us when the mayor and the archbishop arrived. The archbishop had a Cadillac limousine and was given to arriving as the last guest of importance at events. My father much admired the archbishop, but that night it was my father's intention that I should arrive after His Grace.

We did this with respect, but we were mindful that the archbishop had declined to rule on whether I, as a non-Catholic but yet a member of the High School Catholic League Champion Football Team, could represent the church as one of the Catholic All-Stars in the game that had been played the previous evening. By declining to make the ruling, the archbishop had left the decision to the coach of the Catholic All-Stars, Coach Madinger. The coach, a devout member of Opus Dei, had started a controversy at the end of the season by declaring that as a non-Catholic, I could not play for the Catholic All-Stars. That I had been voted an All-Star by sports reporters across the state of Alabama mattered not to him. My teachers, all Jesuits, suspected Coach Madinger of political intrigue in his motives, but then the Jesuits did not care for Opus Dei members, so their suspicions might just have been, well, Jesuitical. I had my own suspicions that eventually several of them, with whom my father had been friends since his days in the local Catholic orphanage, might have been responsible for the final solution to the problem.

Rob Boulanger, the coach of the Public School All-Stars, was a devout Catholic. He belonged to St. Matthew's parish. The pastor of St. Matthew's, Father O'Shea, was a Jesuit, like my teachers. After my father's appeal to the archbishop was declined, Coach Boulanger offered to allow me to play for the Public School All-Stars. Coach Madinger could not say no, or it would have appeared his decision might have in some way been personal.

So instead of taking the field in the gold-and-black uniform of the Catholic All-Stars, I had run onto the field wearing the red-and-white uniform of the Public School All-Stars. I had played the game well above my ability because moral indignation had been a great motivator. I made fourteen unassisted tackles and thirteen assisted, and I intercepted a pass. We held a team favored by two and a half touchdowns to a 0–0 tie. It was a moral victory of the highest order. Some might have ascribed my performance to the fact I had played the entire just-ended season on the same team as the majority of players who were now on the other side of the ball, but, as we all understand, knowledge of an opposing game plan is one thing; execution of an effective counterattack is another. At least that was what my father told me, and my father had, in the fourteen years I had known him, seldom been wrong.

The car was there. I did the best I could to help my mother into her wrap. People followed us out on the porch. The car was magnificent. It was a steel-blue 1934 Cadillac Fleetwood. It was the kind of car that would have taken Clark Gable to the premier of *Gone with the Wind*. We had a chauffeur and a footman. I recognized both. The chauffeur was Lamar, who worked at the Star Taxi Company. The footman was Boudreaux, a doorman at the Café Royale. Boudreaux was holding the back door open. I allowed Aunt Betty and my mother to enter first. I sat on the right so I could exit first and then extend my left hand to assist my mother and Aunt Betty as they left the car. I wondered how we were going to know when the archbishop had arrived, but the crackle of the taxi radio under the dash quickly provided the answer. Why did I think that radio might also have the police bands on it?

The country club was like many others built in the 1920s. It had large windows across the front facing the portico. Thus everyone would have seen the archbishop arrive and be greeted by the mayor, who, as a member of the congregation of the Basilica of the Immaculate Conception, would never have arrived after the archbishop. They would be having cocktails in the gathering room, which was at the front of the building; so when we pulled up, all would see us.

The car stopped in the full light of the portico. Boudreaux jumped out and opened the rear door. As I exited he touched his cap. I was loving this. I turned and offered my left hand to my mother as she stepped out of the car and then to Aunt Betty. Boudreaux closed the door and quickly moved to the front door of the country club. With my mother gingerly placing her hand through the crook of my right elbow and my aunt taking my left arm, we strode through the doors held open by Boudreaux, who once again touched the brim of his cap. Everyone inside turned to stare.

I was sure they were staring at me, but truth be known, my mother, at thirty-eight, and my aunt Betty, a year younger, were beautiful women.

Both teams and their families were there. The Catholics wore their navy-blue school blazers and light-gray trousers. It was the uniform. The public-school boys were in a variety of sport coats, although some wore suits. All looked ill at ease in ties. Like the Catholics I wore a navy-blue blazer, but that night it wasn't the cotton twill uniform of my schoolmates. Rather it was a light worsted wool onto which my mother had sewn a specially made school crest woven of bullion metal thread. Instead of light-gray trousers, I was wearing charcoal-gray, cuffed trousers over well-polished black oxfords that contrasted significantly with my colleagues' oxblood loafers. My black-and-gold school tie was perfectly centered between the narrow spread collars of a new, white broadcloth shirt. Its French cuffs were secured by gold links that, like the buttons on my blazer, bore the seal of the Confederacy.

My father and I had gone over my presentation since late the previous night. I had risen at five that morning and had sat in my chair for two hours, sipping strong black coffee and visualizing how I would act and what I would say. At seven my father had called me into his bedroom, where we worked on my speech for another two hours. We didn't write it out. We just made it up and practiced it.

"Short!" my father kept emphasizing. "Keep it short! Acknowledgments first. The archbishop over the mayor, over the school president, over the public-school superintendent.

Don't forget the players, both sides. It isn't necessary for you to thank the parents. Others before you will have done that."

By nine o'clock that morning, I was ready for the evening. My father, however, was not. He was on the phone the rest of the morning making the arrangements, most of which I've already described. It was after that I decided to do what I would do later.

As I was being introduced to the archbishop and his shadow, the mayor, I took my right hand casually out of my blazer pocket so they could observe the swollen purple mass it had become. I did not want them to think I was slighting them in any manner by offering them my left versus my right hand. I put the swollen hand gently back into the pocket. It hurt to move it, but I was too young, Dr. Davis had said, for painkillers. What were his words? "Tough it out, kiddo. It will pass." Dr. Davis had delivered me fourteen years ago, and I didn't know how many times I'd heard, "Tough it out, kiddo." He'd said the same thing when I had the mumps, chicken pox, measles, and a whole host of broken and dislocated bones. He'd given me a book on Stoicism to read when I was ten. My father had laughed and then encouraged me to read the book.

The archbishop was solicitous but only a little. The mayor kept laying his hand on my right forearm. He was a toucher, a pure politician all the way. Hadn't he seen my hand? What the heck did he think it was connected to? Other people gathered round. If I hadn't been careful, my left hand would have started swelling from shaking so many other hands. Luckily we finally were called in for dinner.

I did not eat. I had filled up on good food at home, know-ing the evening's meal would be a typical country-club chicken or beef menu. It wasn't that the food was bad. It just wasn't… well, it just wasn't food you would expect on the Gulf Coast. Where were the snapper, crab, and shrimp? What about grits and gumbo? The rolls were white and bland. The tea was weak, and the coffee was merely colored water. I'd seen darker water come out of the artesian wells by the bay. Too young to drink, I couldn't even sit there and sip a cocktail.

After the meal the festivities began. The archbishop blessed us. The mayor exhorted us. The heads of schools talked about student athletes and academics. The coaches were thanked but not asked to speak. *Thank God!* Next came the introduction of the local newspaper's sports editor. His speech was a recap of the game. A game, he said, that was unlike any he had seen in his years covering the All-Stars. He had never, he claimed, seen a game as exciting as the previous night's 0–0 tie. His telling of the game was exhilarating. I had no idea we had been so entertaining. His recap was good. We were up, we were down, and we were up again. Running left, running right, throwing down the center of the field. Titans of defense rose up on both sides, slamming the offense to the ground and taking away the ball. Never, he said, had a tie been more exciting. He did not mention that the Catholic All-Stars had been two-and-a-half-touchdown favorites.

Then, just as the crescendo of his story—the part about the titans of defense—began to ebb, I heard my name. He had segued directly from his thrilling recap into the award for the most valuable player. The applause was nice but restrained. There were no shouts of "way to go!" or "good job!" Just room-temperature applause. I was, after all, the youngest player there and the only freshman. That year there would be no announcement by the MVP of which college he would attend. No cheers from the Alabama, Auburn, or sometimes Notre Dame alumni at the tables.

The trophy was a base-metal football, painted gold and mounted on a smallish wooden box. Affixed to the front of the box was a brass plate. The presenter tried to hand me the trophy and shake my hand at the same time. I did not remove my right hand from my pocket, so he eventually saw the problem and put the trophy on the table. Taking my left hand, he directed me to "smile for the photographer."

My turn: acknowledgments. "Your Grace, Mr. Mayor, et cetera, et cetera." Of course, I didn't say *et cetera*. "Some game, wasn't it? I don't think I've ever been quite so much in the zone as I was last night." I thanked my teammates and noted how good the Catholic team was. I couldn't say I'd see them, the Catholics that is, in my classes on Monday because they were all seniors, and I was a freshman. But I did say, "See you in school on Monday." I thanked my father and said, "He can't be here tonight because he suffers from a blood disease. Not enough white blood [*cough, cough*], or is it red blood cells? I forget." This, of course, was not the speech my father and I had planned. Well, most of it was, but I had ad-libbed the last part. I closed by reaching down and grasping the trophy between the football and box, holding it up, and saying, *"Nosce te ipsum."* This, of course—*know thyself*—went over the heads of most, but it was aimed at the Catholics and the archbishop. Coach Madinger might have understood, and if he did, so much the better.

Photographers wanted pictures of me with the archbishop and the trophy, me with the mayor and the trophy, and so forth. But after the picture with the mayor, I apologized and, using my father's illness as the excuse, gathered my ladies and headed for the front door. Lamar had to do some fancy driving, but he got our car into the portico ahead of the archbishop's, so guess who had to wait? I handed Boudreaux the trophy as I got into the backseat. He closed the door and got in the front, and we were off. As my father often said, "Come late, so they anticipate you; leave early, so they will want more."

At home I recounted the evening. It had gone as planned. My mother didn't tell my father about my little dig about the blood. He would learn it from the waiters and others who got it. When he did learn about it, I could count on receiving a homily about "sleeping dogs" or some such. Regrettably, my ad-lib remarks probably went over the heads of those for whom they had been intended.

With everyone gone, my father and I were alone. We sat in the living room. Someone had laid a fire in the grate. It crackled and spit flaming bits of pine against the fire screen, as if in disdain for the dark and humid chill it pushed back.

"Guess who called you tonight?" My father's voice sounded tired.

I answered, "The president. He wants to congratulate me on playing the game well." I did not mean the football game. I smirked.

"No, I think the president has his hands full with the Russians. It was some people from Auburn and a couple of people from Alabama. They're interested in where you might go to college."

I found this amusing since everyone knew I intended to go to West Point, where I would become first captain of the corps.

"Well, I hope you told them I'm not interested. Otherwise they may force a new convertible on me. After I get my driver's license, of course. And then there'll be all those college girls calling me—yuck." I said *yuck* but secretly coveted the opportunity to ride in a convertible with college girls.

My father saw through me in a heartbeat. He said, "Boosters can do a lot for an up-and-coming football player. Especially one who can pass the entrance exams."

Then he drew himself up in his chair, which seemed to become larger every day. "But you know, Jack, you should have a backup plan. Just in case something happens. For example, what if next year it's your leg instead of your finger? What then?" He paused as if to think, but I knew he was catching his breath before saying, "We'll not do it tonight, but we'll discuss this matter soon."

He was tired. On Saturday nights past, we would have stayed up well beyond midnight talking, but that night I could see it was an effort for him even to rise from the chair. I did not offer to help. He wouldn't have liked it.

In my room I sat in my chair, feet crossed on the ottoman. The small carriage clock on my desk pinged 1:00 a.m. I had been sitting there more than two hours. I had been pondering the Latin phrase my father had suggested I use to end my speech. Translated it was, "Know thyself." It made sense, but I wasn't completely sure I understood how it applied to winning an award and overcoming discrimination.

But mostly I was worried about my father. His behavior concerned me. He had always been there. I was simply an adjunct. I was what I was and who I was because he gave me form and thought. I stood not in his shadow but in the light reflected from his personality. And it was that reflected light that allowed me to cast my own shadow. The previous day I had been a demigod. That dark, chilly December Sunday morning, I had reverted to my mortal form of child. Not demigod, not man, but child. What should I do? What could I do? What would I do?

And as always I assured myself with the thought, *I will ask my father. He will know.*

May 1962

CHAPTER 6

A KEENER EDGE

"AND NOW BATTING…Batting…batting…" The an-
nouncer's voice trailed away as it echoed round the cavernous
ballpark. "NUMBER TWELVE…Twelve…twelve…JACK
JOURDAIN…Jourdain…Jourdain…"

As the imaginary scene unfolded, the crowd applauded;
some cheered. From the dugout my teammates shouted, "Get a
hit, Jack! Hit's a run, babe, hit's a run!"

Runner on third, score tied, nothing to nothing, bottom of
the ninth, two out. "And on the mound for the Dodgers is their
six-foot-six rocket-throwing ace, Don Drysdale. He is throwing a two-hitter…"

I approached the plate, looking at the third-base coach. It
was already decided what we would do, but I wanted to make
sure the runner on third knew. The coach gave the sign. I ac-
knowledged it by adjusting my batting helmet. I stepped into
the batter's box. I held my left hand up to show the umpire I
was still getting ready. I dug in. I checked the infield. They
were back. Of course they were back; they didn't have to worry

about the runner at third, but they had to get me out, so we'd go to extra innings.

I crowded the plate from the left-hand side. I got in even closer than normal. I wanted Drysdale to throw it inside. I wanted him to demonstrate to me that the plate was his, and I shouldn't crowd it. Pitchers can't stand for batters to try to take the plate away from them. He would throw it inside to brush me back.

I knew Drysdale wanted me off the plate. He shook off the first sign the catcher gave him. It was probably a curve ball. I didn't hit the curve as well as other pitches, and the catcher knew it. He was calling to win the game, but Drysdale needed me off the plate. He was going to throw heat, and it was coming inside. The catcher must have agreed, because Drysdale checked the runner on third and started into his stretch. As he rocked on his heel to throw, I opened my front foot away from the plate and then slid my left hand just a smidgen up the barrel of the bat. I scooted forward six inches in the batter's box.

The runner on third was breaking. I could see him in my mind's eye. The catcher saw him too. All good catchers have a sixth sense for knowing these things; in the mind of the catcher, he knew exactly what was coming, and there was nothing he could do about it.

Drysdale strode forward. Coming almost off the pitcher's mound, he looked like Zeus hurling a lightning bolt. And while it was only traveling about ninety-six miles an hour, you could have easily convinced me it was the speed of light. But I wasn't really worried about the speed. It was slipping contact that I wanted, outside to inside, left to right. When the ball reached the plate, I was already half a step toward first. Just as I had wanted, the ball was inside and thigh high. I loosened my hold on the bat to absorb the force of the ball while I pushed the bat left to right with my left hand.

At that point it became a race. The ball rolled down the first-base line, staying on the grass. Drysdale came off the mound, but his huge pitching stride had taken him too much toward the plate. The ball was by him. The first baseman broke in, but he was playing behind the bag, and he was slow. The second baseman ran to cover first base, but it wouldn't be close because he had been at his regular depth. On a normal bunt, it would have been the catcher and me. And the catcher was Johnny Roseboro, the Dodgers' best. But with a runner breaking for home off third, Johnny had to cover the plate.

As the runner crossed home, and I—deep in my imagined glory—stood triumphantly on first, the imagined crowd anointed us with shouting and applause that was as palpable as that first wave of humidity on a midsummer day on the Gulf Coast.

"Need some more ice, Boy?" my father asked. *Boy* is my family name. It had started with my grandfather calling me Boy and referring to me in the third person as "the boy." Later, in the family, everyone called me Boy.

"No thanks, Dad. There are still some cubes floating in the bowl." All too abruptly back in the real world, I looked down at my left hand soaking in the large mixing bowl my mother used for bread dough. There was a purplish hue developing at the base of my thumb and forefinger. If it weren't for the numbness the ice was causing, I suspected it would hurt.

My father walked over and lifted my hand out of the water. "So this is the result of your experiment in using a reinforced first baseman's glove as a catcher's mitt? I'd have to say it's back to the drawing board."

He was right. I'd been trying to get away from the over-padded catcher's mitt and find something more flexible to use, but Bishop had been throwing hard that day. I kept catching the ball in the pocket instead of the webbing. The idea of using a first baseman's glove had seemed a good one, but it hadn't worked.

My dad placed my hand back in the bowl. "It's not bad, considering how hard Marvin was throwing today." He always referred to my teammates by their Christian names.

I looked up at him from my reading chair. Well, it was my reading chair, but I might as well have called it my dreaming chair or imagining chair or, as my dad preferred to call it, the visualizing chair. My dad and I were great visualizers. He used it for business and to help manage his illness. I used it for sports and, of course, for imagining my future.

"Yes, sir, he threw hard. But that's about all he did. He's sixteen, Dad. You'd think he would have developed a decent breaking ball by now. I mean, his curve ball doesn't move more than an inch or two. Not far enough so the batter can't get wood on it."

"And how far does your curve ball break?" My father smiled as he asked the question.

He knew I didn't have a curve ball. I was a catcher. If a ball curves when a catcher throws it, somebody invariably misses it, and the catcher gets an error.

"You should work with him on his mechanics," my father instructed. "For example, when you call a curve, he should change his position on the pitching rubber. That changes his delivery, and for certain the scouts will pick up on it." He said the last over his shoulder as he headed slowly across our small hall toward the living room.

Why hadn't I seen that? That was my job. I was the catcher. I was the field general. I deployed the troops. I knew what the opposing batters' strengths and weaknesses were. I called the pitches. Why hadn't I seen that?

That was enough ice water. My hand hadn't been that cold since my father and I had gone to New York City in December 1958. That had been, let's see, three and a half years earlier. He had been a lot healthier then. I dried my hand; it remained numb to the touch. I took the bowl to the kitchen and emptied it in the sink. First a heart attack, and then leukemia. You'd think God would have given a break to a guy who'd been taken from his mother and raised in an orphanage. But then, what did I really know about God? I was a good Episcopalian. I went to Mass, I learned my catechism, I prayed (well, at least at meals), but what did I really know about God?

My father wasn't mad at God, even though I thought he should have been. He took most things in stride, although I did see him become agitated when people used certain derogatory words to describe people of other races or religions. Most times he held his tongue. Sometimes, though, he gave them a sound verbal thrashing. If there was one thing my father was really good at, it was verbally thrashing someone. He had the skill to cut them up into bait so small you could catch only minnows with it. I loved my father, but I hated his disease, and if God didn't come through and do something for the good guys, I was going to hate God as well.

Returning to my room, I turned the radio on as I plopped myself back into my chair. It was warm, but then it was Mobile, and it was May. Mardi Gras and the Azalea Festival were done. We'd finish school by the end of the month. Baseball was going to occupy most of my time that summer. I would also have an increased number of meetings with Mr. Rush, the tutor my father had gotten me. I had switched from a public to a private school for my freshman year, and staying in the top part of the class at the new school was much more difficult. My father said a tutor would improve my performance and increase my chances for a West Point appointment. He was right.

I slowly spun the dial on the Zenith Transoceanic radio next to my chair. It was an old set my father had picked up in a used-furniture store. He had taken it to one of his clients, who replaced the tubes. After that I could pull in stations from all over the world. Not, of course, that I could understand them, although I did pretty well in French, and my father had been working with me on some Italian.

I went to all the clear channels I knew. WLS, WSM, WWL and the like. Generally I could get a baseball game on Sunday evening. I had already listened to the news, but sometimes, when I got the New York or the London stations, I'd listen again. I stopped the dial on WCBS, New York. Sometimes they did the Yankee games. I must have been getting a good bounce off the ionosphere because I could hear clearly. Nope, not baseball, but just as I reached for the dial, I heard:

"Yes, it was a most moving speech. Best I've heard in years. General MacArthur at his best."

Well, as anyone who knew me understood, General MacArthur was one of my heroes. He was right up there with Robert E. Lee, J. E. B. Stuart, Roy Campanella, and Yogi Berra. I sat up in my chair. The commentators were speaking about the General. I glanced at the autographed photograph in the frame on my desk. I was shaking hands with the General outside the Waldorf-Astoria in New York City. That was a story from what seemed many years ago. Wait, what was that the man had just said? I fiddled with the gain switch slightly.

"—speech at West Point. The quality is a little grainy, but you can hear the General perfectly well. We understand this is the only recording of the General's speech, and we'll play it for you now. So here it is—General MacArthur's speech yesterday evening to the corps of cadets at West Point…"

I sat up straight. I slid forward onto the front six inches of my chair, almost as if I was a plebe sitting at attention. I listened to the General:

"As I was leaving the hotel this morning, the doorman asked me, 'Where are you bound for, Sir?' When I replied, 'West Point,' he remarked, 'It's a beautiful place. Have you ever been there before?'"

That's Mick, I thought. *The doorman at the Waldorf is named Michael, but the General calls him Mick. It's got to be Mick.* This was too good to be true. Maybe I was imagining it. No, I was in the real world. It was on the radio. I listened closely.

"Duty, Honor, Country: Those three hallowed words reverently dictate what you ought to be, what you can be, and what you will be. They are your rallying points to build courage when courage seems to fail, to regain faith when there seems to be little cause for faith, to create hope when hope becomes forlorn...

"The code which those words perpetuate embraces the highest moral law and will stand the test of any ethics or philosophies ever promoted for the uplift of mankind. Its requirements are for the things that are right, and its restraints are from the things that are wrong...

"Today marks my final roll call with you. I want you to know that when I cross the river, my last conscious thoughts will be of the Corps and the Corps and the Corps."[1]

I did not move. How long I sat I do not know. The General's words echoed in my brain like the announcer's voice over the loud speakers: *DUTY......Duty.......duty...HONOR...Honor... honor...COUNTRY...Country...country.* If only God could speak so clearly. If only God would deign to speak to us again as General MacArthur had. But suddenly I knew I had my guide-posts. I must do that which was right. I must do the right thing and avoid the wrong thing. The yardstick I must use to measure my actions was the set of words *duty, honor, country.*

I could sit no longer. I sprinted to find my father. He was in the living room—a short sprint of some six steps away. He was sitting in his chair. There was a record on the stereo. It was French jazz. His eyes were closed. My father sang with the record. *"Plus bleu que tes yeux..."* It was one of his Patachou albums. He liked her voice; he thought it was stronger than Edith Piaf's. His voice, however, was somewhat reedy these days. He stopped to catch his breath.

I never interrupted my father when he was listening to music. It was one of his pleasures. He had so few left to him these days. I should have sat and waited, but I couldn't. I could wait, but I couldn't sit.

---

1 General Douglas MacArthur's speech to the Corps of Cadets at the U.S. Military Academy at West Point, NY on May 12, 1962 in accepting the Thayer Award. http://penelope.uchicago.edu

How did he do it? How did he know? I had been quiet, but he rose, crossed to the stereo, and took the needle off the record. Normally he would have gone to the mantel and filled his pipe from the humidor, but he no longer smoked, not even his pipe. He returned to his chair. I saw that even the effort of rising and crossing the room had taxed his energy reserves. He was much thinner now, and he seemed shorter. Yes, of course I had grown taller, but my father seemed to be shrinking.

"How's the hand?" he asked almost breathlessly.

I looked at my hand. My formerly frozen hand that I hadn't thought about for the last hour. There was a dark-purple patch between the thumb and forefinger.

"Doesn't hurt at all," I answered. I was concerned. I wondered if I should get my mother. But then, as if he had caught up with his breath, he smiled. His old baritone voice was back.

"So if it's not your hand falling off, which I imagined you might want to consult me on, what's got you twitching like a drop of water on a hot skillet?" My father had more expressions than anyone I knew. I could never learn them all.

I tried to synopsize the General's speech coherently. As my father listened, his head was in his left hand, and his elbow was on the chair's arm. I was pacing the living room floor, and my hand hammered into my palm in emphasis whenever I pronounced *duty, honor, country*. I ended with, "It's the answer! Do the right thing!"

My father shifted his position in the chair. It seemed a much bigger chair these days.

"Yes, Jack, it is the answer. It has always been the answer. But let me ask you this. How do you know what the right thing is?"

I was deflated, but I rallied. "You have to use the measuring stick of duty, honor, country."

He responded with a voice still strong. "But those things are concepts, ideas that have no substance. We can grasp them only in our minds as abstractions. Actions, on the other hand, have substance; they have consequence. How do you measure a substantive deed against an abstract idea?"

My enthusiasm drained. I didn't know how to answer the question. I know my face showed my disappointment.

"Duty, honor, and country are concepts you integrate into your life," my father continued. "They are like faith. They cannot be seen, but they are the cornerstones upon which your structure as a human being is being built. Trust me: they are already firmly built into your foundation. You need only to continue to understand that since they are part of your makeup, you need to learn to rely on yourself, on your own judgment, and not that of others. Do you remember what was carved above the entrance to the temple of the oracle at Delphi?"

I did remember and told him, "Know thyself."

"Yes. Know thyself. Because if you know yourself, you already have the answer you need. One never needs to enter the temple to get the correct answer. And you never need look further than yourself to know whether you are doing the right thing. Just remember the right thing is almost always not the easy thing. If you do the wrong thing, you'll know. Then you need to correct it as quickly as possible. If you're wrong, admit it.

Learn from your mistake, and move on. But you are correct; the answer is 'do the right thing.' And I know you will." He leaned back, almost out of breath again, exhausted from the homily.

My enthusiasm had returned, but it had been tempered like hot steel plunged into cold water. The General and my father forged me as a Damascene smith might have shaped a blade. I was a harder, stronger substance that would take a keener edge.

April 1965

CHAPTER 7

DUTY

THE SMALL CARRIAGE CLOCK PINGED midnight. I loved the sound. Unlike the mantel clock in the living room, the ring did not carry beyond my bedroom. It was an ancient clock. Well, ancient to me. My grandfather had given it to me when I was ten. He'd discovered it among the life detritus of an old maid cousin who'd died of a broken heart at the age of ninety. He told me the story one Christmas afternoon as we sat in front of his sitting-room fireplace.

Engaged to the love of her life in 1916, Cousin Sue agreed to wait for James, her fiancé, to finish medical school. Then they agreed to wait for James's army service in the Great War to end. Upon his return home from France, they planned a grand wedding for the spring of 1919. Lucky in war, James was not so lucky in peace. He died ministering to patients during the great flu pandemic early in the year. Sixty-five years later, she died of a broken heart, never having married. It was a sad story, which fit my mood that night.

I tried to find guidance in the story of Cousin Sue and the inscription engraved at the base of her fluted silver clock: *"Tempus fugit, memento mori."* Time is fleeting, remember that you must die. Obviously time had not flown for her, although she had certainly died. I'm sure she'd thought of the inscription every day. My grandfather told me she'd become a nurse and went to China as a medical missionary for the Presbyterian Church. She was there when the Japanese invaded in 1937. She had an incredibly eventful and useful life. It was the kind of life Ernest Hemingway would have written about, if he could have written about women as something other than appendages to men. But still, they say, she died of a broken heart.

I looked again at the letter in my lap. It started out with "Dear Jean." That was my real name. Jack was only a nickname. "I am pleased to offer you an appointment to the United States Military Academy…"

It had been more than two weeks since the letter had arrived, and I had only two days left to accept or decline. If I accepted the appointment, I would need to report for "Beast Barracks" at West Point at the end of June. Over on my desk were letters from Princeton, Alabama, Sewanee, and a number of other universities. They all offered me scholarships if I would attend. How astonishingly lucky I was. And yet not so lucky.

I had spoken the day before to Dr. Davis, our family physician. This was our fortieth or so conversation in the past five years, and, for the fortieth or so time, he told me the same thing. The cancer doctor gave my father six months to live. Of course he had given my father six months to live five years ago when he'd discovered the leukemia. In other words, he had no idea.

My thinking chair seemed too small that night. I had grown, but the chair, a sturdy leather club chair, was capable of supporting much larger frames than mine. Perhaps the chair wasn't too small physically for me. Maybe the confinement I felt was from some other source.

The night's distraction would not, alas, end with the equanimity of other perplexing nights. I could not simply convince myself that I would seek assistance from my father in the morning and go to bed for the sleep of the virtuous. I knew my father wanted me to go to West Point. We had discussed it for years. He had hired a tutor to help me prepare. I had told everyone that I would go there and that I would become first captain.

We had the journey planned. My father and I would fly from Mobile to Atlanta and from Atlanta to New York City. We would go up early to catch a Yankees game. On my appointed arrival day at West Point, my father and I would take a train from Grand Central Station up the Hudson Valley to Peerskill. He would put me in a taxi, and we would say goodbye at the station. "A young gentleman should never have to arrive at his college with parents in tow." Or so said my father. I reminded him that not only had MacArthur arrived at West Point with his mother in tow, but she had taken up residence in a nearby boarding house and stayed for his entire academy career.

"That may be so," he said, "but your mother and I have more confidence in you than Mrs. MacArthur did in Douglas."

Thinking about a train trip up the Hudson Valley made me even sadder. My father and I had traveled by train from Mobile to New York City five—no, almost six years earlier. We saw the New York Giants play the Baltimore Colts in "The Greatest Game Ever Played." At least that was what the press called it. We were too cold to make judgments on the game at the time, but my presence at the game continued to garner significant prestige for me among my peers. I remembered the trip well, not because of the game but because I met General of the Army Douglas MacArthur. I looked at the picture on my desk of a young boy shaking hands with an old man. In the background was Michael, the uniformed doorman at the Waldorf-Astoria, who was a really nice man. The General had died a year before. I didn't know where Michael was. The General had called him Mick.

Perhaps I should have written Mick, care of the Waldorf. Maybe he was still there. But he would probably have told me the General would say, "Do what you think is right." I already knew that was what the General would have said. "Do what you think is right."

My father said, "Go to West Point. It is your destiny."

My tutor, Mr. Rush, said, "You are almost a grown man. You must make your own decision. I have every confidence you will make the correct one."

My mother said, "Do what your heart tells you is the right thing." Only my mother believed decisions are made with your heart, not your head.

In truth I was only seventeen. I was not fully grown, although at five feet, ten inches, and 185 pounds I probably couldn't have expected to grow much more physically. Everybody expected me to make the "right" decision. I knew doing the right thing was a difficult proposition, although, I admit, when I first heard it expounded as the basic tool for decision making, I thought it would be easy. I suppose that was because my reference point was my father, who always, it seemed, made the right decision. I never knew how hard it was to decide what was most right. It turned out doing the thing was much easier than deciding what to do.

Parts of the decision were easy. Alabama was out. I was a good football player, but Alabama was the national champion. I might have made the team, but they'd have people who were bigger, faster, and almost as knowledgeable about football as I was. It was only a couple of hundred miles away, but it might as well have been Princeton, which was a full day away, and that was if you could afford to fly. Sewanee was the same—a full day's car trip from Mobile. Tulane was closer, but I'd still have to live in New Orleans.

I walked over to my desk and sorted through the letters. I stopped at the one from Spring Hill College right there in Mobile. It offered a full scholarship. They wanted me to play baseball; they didn't have a football team. I had watched Spring Hill play baseball all my life. I liked their purple hats with the Gothic *S* on the front. My father had friends from his years in the orphanage who had become teaching brothers in the Jesuits. Some of them taught at Spring Hill, which wasn't really the college's name. Formally it was The Jesuit University of the South, but everybody called it Spring Hill College—because it was on Spring Hill Road, I guess.

If I went there, I could live right in my same bedroom. I could keep my business, which, considering that my father's working ability had dropped off, helped with the niceties my mother's salary didn't cover. It was a dirty business, but I never lacked work, and I'd already hired two part-time employees. My father kept my books, when he was able. He liked to bother people with phone calls when they hadn't paid their bills. I told him not to worry. If I didn't show up to clean their restrooms for a couple of days, they began to lose business. People often did a double take when I told them what I did. "That's right, I clean toilets. Not just any toilets but gas station toilets." It was easier for the managers to pay me than to force their gas jockeys to clean rooms that could quickly take on an odor as foul as that of the Augean stables—although I'd have to say that if the Greek poets had ever experienced the smell of a gas station restroom, they might not have thought the Augean stables smelled that bad.

I read the Spring Hill letter again. It was a straightforward offer. I couldn't help but smile at the signature. The head of admissions was Brother Timothy G. Fink. Fink was a funny name. I remembered Mike Fink and the river pirates in Walt Disney's *Davy Crockett* movie. That movie had been a long time ago—more than half my life.

I turned the ceiling fan from high to low, turned off the table lamp, parted the mosquito net, and slid beneath the ironed sheets on my bed. They were cool for the moment, but I was a furnace when I slept. By the time I woke, the sheets would be soaked with sweat, and I would be cold in the humid air of an April morning.

The night was quiet. I wondered if I should pray. I had been praying strenuously for five years, but I didn't think God was listening. I had talked about this with Father Kinepp, who said that maybe God actually was listening and answering. Maybe that was why my father had lived four and a half years past the six months his doctors had given him in 1960. I didn't know. It wasn't, I didn't think, what I'd been praying for. Maybe I should have paid more attention to what I was asking for when I prayed. Sometimes I felt guilty. Was I praying for my father, or was I praying for myself? If I was praying for myself and God was answering by keeping my father alive in weakness and pain, was I sinning? Could God have been so cruel just to teach me a lesson?

I also felt guilty because I only half believed in God. If God didn't exist then prayer had absolutely no bearing on my father's health. If God did exist, I still wondered whether what I did or said had any effect. Either way, it was difficult to accept that my father could have been given so many troubles in so short a life.

My father didn't agree. He pointed out all the good he had. He didn't dwell on the bad. Without bad, he said, you couldn't appreciate the good. He was a Christian Stoic, a true believer. He would have done well, if doing well had been a possibility, in the Colosseum facing Nero's lions and tigers. I wouldn't have. I would have been trying to climb the walls to go after Nero.

I tried to practice the Stoic meditation my father used. I don't know if it worked, but I fell asleep.

The clock lightly struck five. Its small silver bell had a resonating euphony. Time to get ready for school.

My father sat in his chair in the living room. He was swaddled in his dressing gown. His slippers were too large for his feet. His head was almost lost in the collar of the gown, which rose above his back like a cowl. His face was drawn, but the wayward curl hung over his left eye, and, remarkably, his hair remained full and black. His eyes didn't twinkle, but they were alive. Between the eyes and the curl, I could just make out the rakish pirate master he might have been.

A cup of coffee sat on the teak occasional table to his left. Its steam rose in the humidity. The half-light of morning seeped through the partially closed plantation shutters, creating a pattern of light and dark bars on the floor. In the back of my mind, I saw the bars as though they made the living room his prison.

I did not have coffee, preferring to take my early morning caffeine in the form of an RC Cola. I also had two doughnuts from the close-by Malbis bakery. They delivered fresh bread and doughnuts three times a week. That day I had a vanilla glazed and an orange glazed. I plopped on the couch.

"Enjoy them while you can," my father said.

"Enjoy what them?" I asked.

"The doughnuts and RC. You won't get them at the academy."

"Yes, sir, you're right. I believe they eat all sorts of healthy food, like eggs and bacon and such. Why, they probably serve— what was that head sausage we had in Maryland? Scrabble?"

"I think you mean scrapple."

"Right, scrapple."

"Did you answer the letter?" No beating around the bush with my father.

"No, sir, not yet. I haven't decided."

"Jack, there is no decision to be made. You made it years ago. This is what you have wanted forever. Sign the paper, and send it back."

"Dad, we all agreed this is my decision. It's the first time I will make a life-changing decision on my own. I have to be sure. I have to feel it's the right thing."

"Jack, it is the right thing. Just sign the damn letter." My father never cursed unless he was thoroughly frustrated. His illness had increased his frustration levels. "I want you to sign the letter. I want to know before I die that we succeeded."

That was the absolute first time my father had mentioned dying. He had always affirmed life. Dying was part of life, but it was something we never discussed. You simply accepted it and went on with your own life. When my grandfather died, we didn't talk about death, even though we were in the room at his home when he died. When others died, it was almost always offstage, as they say on Broadway.

"Dad, I will make the right decision. If it isn't right, then I'll admit I'm wrong and do something else. But I will make the choice that is right according to the information I have. It's all I can do. And as for succeeding, we've already done that. Shall I go and fetch all the letters from my desk? We've won the option of a paid college education. That, dear father, is success."

I chugged the last of my RC and stepped across the room to kiss him good-bye. As I leaned over, the odor of sickness assailed me. His breath smelled of undigested medicine and bile. His blood vessels created a red-and-blue road map underneath tightly drawn, yellowed, paper-thin skin. His ears appeared too large for his head. I kissed him on his forehead as he had done to me so many times before. He was clammy and cool. That was why he spoke of dying. That was what death looked and smelled like.

I retreated to my room, gathered up my book bag, stuffed it with the letters from the colleges, and went out through the back door. Out to my car. I sat behind the wheel and cried.

My final in calculus was easy. My teacher didn't demand that we show our work. He was only interested in results. He would, however, stop us in the middle of the test and ask us to answer separate questions. He called me up after the first twenty minutes. Everyone else kept working. I was the fifth student he had called to the front of the room. He showed me a problem.

"Mr. Jourdain, would you please answer this question?" Not "could you answer" but "would you answer." He had great confidence in his teaching abilities. I did the problem and gave him the answer. He smiled and marked me off in his book. Before I left his desk, he said, "Mr. Jourdain, please know that all of us here are sick in our hearts about your father. He is such a good man. I'm sure God has a special place reserved for him."

I could only mutter, "Thank you, Brother."

I had no other tests that day. The rest of school was lunch and study hall. I sat and wrote letters to the colleges. My penmanship was good, and I had an excellent fountain pen with a fine calligraphy point. They were short. "Thank you, but…" kinds of letters. I addressed envelopes and then asked Brother Joseph if I might be excused to mail my answers to the colleges. He agreed and, as he gave me the hall pass, asked, "Now, Jack, where have you chosen? West Point, no doubt."

"Well, Brother Joseph, you are correct. There is no doubt about West Point."

The post office was close by, and it took little time to buy the stamps and mail the letters. Shoving them in the box, I felt relieved. Too late to second-guess. They were off, and tampering with the US mail was a federal offense. I had no restroom to clean that afternoon. I did stop, however, at a pay phone to make sure the two college students I had hired part time showed up at the appropriate gas stations to take care of their facilities.

I had one more stop to make. The day was nice. A perfect spring day. Well, as perfect as spring days got on the Gulf Coast, where spring could mean it was just in the eighties instead of the nineties. I put the top down on the Willys Jeepster I had bought from my uncle Gale. It had been a mess when he'd gotten it, but it had cleaned up pretty well; it was a nice utilitarian white with red-plastic upholstery, and I didn't mind carrying around toilet-cleaning supplies in it. It was not the car I wanted, but it was the one I needed. It was the right decision. One more stop, and I'd go home.

I entered through the front door, my book bag slung over my shoulder. I was wearing my school uniform of khaki trousers, white shirt, school tie, and navy-blue cotton blazer. The sole of one of my Bass Weejuns was held in place by white athletic tape wrapped around the top and bottom. I was wearing a purple baseball cap with a Gothic *S*.

My father was once again in his chair. He was now dressed in a long-sleeved print shirt and khaki pants. He was wearing a cotton cardigan sweater against the chill of his illness. He was still, however, wearing his too-big elk-skin slippers. He had been reading and had nodded off. There was a book on his lap. He opened his eyes as I closed the door.

I dropped the book bag on the sofa and once again leaned over to kiss his forehead. He smelled of Old Spice and Brylcreem. Much better.

I saw his eyes cut to the hat then to my eyes. Once again he locked those black eyes into my green. Before he could speak, I smiled, saying, "Well, everything is as it should be. I've made the right choice."

He looked at the purple hat and smiled. "If you thought West Point was going to be tough, wait until those college Jesuits get hold of you. Next thing you know, you'll be a soldier in the army of Christ." He pulled me down and kissed me on the forehead.

"By the way," I said, "Brother Timothy sends his respects."

I grinned; he looked sheepish. I'd never, ever seen him look sheepish. Then, ever so slightly, there was a twinkle in his eyes, and the disproportionate ears made him look like a self-satisfied elf.

So, apologies to General MacArthur, I would not be the first captain at West Point. But in no small way he was responsible for my decision. "Duty, honor, country," he had said. First was duty, and I knew where my duty lay. Maybe a real candidate for first captain would have gone to West Point. But then again, maybe he wouldn't. Perhaps I had demonstrated a command decision capability. Time would tell.

Four more years with the Jesuits. I might be a Catholic before it was over. Then again I might not.

In my room the small clock dinged five o'clock and once again reminded me, *"Tempus fugit, memento mori."*

February 1966

CHAPTER 8

HONOR

"It's impossible to prepare for, so why bother?" This advice came from my new best friend.

"Well, we have to stay on top of current events. What if one of the topics deals with something like Vietnam?" I shifted in my Metroliner seat as I tried to refold the *New York Times* op-ed section. "Knowing what some leaders think about it could be important in scoring a point or two." I avoided his eyes, knowing that if he captured me with his gaze, I would be lost and end up playing gin with him.

"Yes, that might be so." His concurrence emboldened me. I generally lost our little impromptu arguments. But then he continued, "That is if you actually consider any of those people leaders. If they were real leaders, they would have had us out of the mess years ago. The very concept of democracy is dependent upon a self-sustaining middle class, and there is no middle class in Vietnam. Thus a democratic government cannot survive. You deal." He shoved the deck of cards across the thin table toward me. I lost again. His logic was unassailable.

He was a force formidable. I thought *formidable* in French. It sounded better.

I shoved the newspaper between my hip and the train seat. Picking up the cards, I began to shuffle. I looked across the table, and it was like looking in a mirror. The same height and weight, the same dark-brown hair, olive skin, and green eyes. Yet there was a difference, like that between a black-and-white movie and a wide-screen Technicolor epic. I was the black and white. He was the Technicolor. Where my skin was a light bronze-olive mix, his was a bold red-olive mix. My eyes were green with slight yellow-brown rings on the insides of the irises. His were a brilliant emerald green with small, bright-gold flecks throughout. There was a depth to the green that seemed to go on forever. His gaze could pull you into the depths of his eyes such that you felt you were falling deeper and deeper into a maelstrom in an emerald-green sea. His eyes were those of a mesmerizer.

Although his people were from down around Bayou La Batre and Biloxi, we both had southern port-city accents, although his *R*s were shorter than mine. When I pronounced *barber*, it came out *barbar*, but he said *barba*. We both played baseball. We were both catchers. We both liked Sazerac cocktails. More importantly, for five years we had shared the same tutor. Finally, but perhaps most importantly, we shared first names. He was Jean-Louis Thibodeaux, and I was Jean Anton Jourdain. There was, however, one thing we didn't share. He was a pushover for a redhead. I, on the other hand, was a push-over for brunettes, blondes, women with raven or auburn hair, and—OK, the occasional redhead. We both preferred women who could speak French or at least Acadian.

"Remember, no cheating," I said as I dealt.

"*Mon cher*, I don't cheat. I just read your mind. That's not cheating." His accent was thick. He did this sometimes when he was having fun or when we had had a drink too many. I looked up, and he had me fixed in that direct stare he used. He arranged his cards. I halfway expected him to lay them all down immediately and claim, "Gin!"

"I know you can't read minds," I said. "At least I'm pretty sure you can't, but still you do something well, or I wouldn't already owe you ten dollars. And we're not yet in Philadelphia."

"Well, if a dollar a hand is too rich for your blood, we could play for shares in your company." He was referring to the cleaning service I had run since my freshman year in high school.

I fixed him with my own stare and said, "Read my mind."

"Jack!" he replied, with mock surprise. "Does your mother know you use such language? And besides, you know I prefer redheads."

We laughed.

"Gin," he said, laying down his cards.

I grimaced, put my cards down, and looked out the window at the snowy terrain. It was amazing how something I disliked so much—and I definitely disliked snow—could change the landscape from junkyards, falling-down houses, and sewage run-off canals to a picture-perfect, tranquil winter countryside awaiting the coming thaw of spring. The snow out there must have been three feet deep, and the temperature had to be below freezing. I dreaded the thought of walking through the canyons of New York City, where the wind demonstrated Bernoulli's principle with great efficacy.

"So Jean-Louis, we're going to stay at your father's townhouse?" I asked because, while I knew Jean-Louis's father was well off, a townhouse in the sixties on the East Side of New York was like—well, where rich people lived.

"In a way," Jean-Louis replied. "It's owned by the *societé* my father is a member of, so he uses it when he comes to New York. Nobody in his right mind wants to come to New York in February, so we can use it as long as we wish—certainly through Sunday, when this competition is over. I'm sure Diaz will put you in a nice room."

"Diaz?"

"Yes, he manages the place. Sort of a butler, maître d'hôtel type, although my father calls him Generalissimo. I think he was some kind of honcho in Cuba before Castro took over."

"Oh."

We arrived at Penn Station and were met at the gate to the platform by a driver holding a placard inscribed "Mr. Thibodeaux." He took us outside, into the freezing gray of a New York late afternoon. There was a limousine waiting at the curb.

A short drive later, there were other people taking my bag out of the trunk. The bag was a midsize leather duffel of some years; my father had found it in a shop when I was five. He took it to his cobbler and asked him to refurbish the brown-gold leather and restitch the corners and such. Then the cobbler embossed another piece of leather with "Jourdain" and sewed it over the gold-embossed initials of the first owner. I planned to give it to my son someday, assuming I had one. I also had a leather suit bag. It didn't match the duffel, but it too had been resurrected to serve again. Have I mentioned how lucky I have been in my life?

I was right. It was freezing outside. Inside, though, it was nice. There was a fire in the fireplace. Imagine that—a fireplace in the middle of Manhattan. It was a rather large fireplace. Then I saw that it was gas. Oh, well. Still, it was a fireplace.

Jean-Louis hadn't mentioned that Diaz had a staff to run the house. It was like a private hotel. The car that had picked us up at the station would take us wherever we wanted or needed to go. So I guessed I wouldn't have to suffer the winds on walks to the subway.

"OK, Bubba." Jean-Louis was standing at the door to my large and too-much bedroom. "How about an early dinner and then maybe catch some jazz?"

"How about we stay in and prepare for the competition tomorrow?" I countered.

"Look, Bubba. It's like this." He leaned against the doorjamb. "They give a topic, and we have fifteen minutes to prepare a five-minute presentation. We did it at college then at the regionals, and now we're going to do the same thing at the nationals. We're either ready or we're not. Besides, this is all gravy. We miss a week and a half of school, we get five nights in New York, and my father has an account at the Café Carlyle."

I wasn't generally this easy, but Jean-Louis did have a point. Either we were ready for this extemporaneous speech contest or we weren't.

Besides, as he'd said, it was all gravy. Nobody expected two freshmen to win at the college level and even less so at the regionals, but there we were. In the finals representing the Southeastern region. So that made us at least the sixth-best team in the country—and that was if we finished last, which I didn't think we'd do. We'd compete individually, but our scores were added together for the team competition. You could get there only as a team, but they did name an individual champion. He or she was introduced before the team champion was named. For example, the individual champion in our regional competition had been from Washington and Lee University. Unfortunately his partner finished somewhere in the twenties. Jean-Louis and I were both in the top five.

"OK, but still an early evening, right?" I asked. "By the way, you know I have to call home. Can I make a collect call from the phone here in the bedroom?"

"Hell, just pick it up and ask the operator to connect you. The societé has some sort of deal with Bell. I'll be down in the living room toasting my feet."

I picked up the receiver and asked a very nice operator to connect me with Walnut 2-9898 in Mobile. My mother answered the phone.

"He's been worried about you," she said. "Today was not a very good day, but I know he wants to talk to you."

"Hey, Boy!" His voice was weak. "How are things in New York?"

"Hey, Dad. Do you remember how cold we were watching the Colts play the Giants in Yankee Stadium?"

He laughed. Not his usual hearty baritone laugh but a wheezy laugh—almost like the cough of someone who was trying to speak and sneeze at the same time.

"That was some cold," he answered.

"Well, Dad, I guess we're just a couple of wimps because that cold was more like a spring day than what it is outside now. Did you know they've got snow piles on all the corners?"

"I hate snow," he said. Like son, like father.

"Yes, sir, I do too. But it's what we've got."

"So when is this competition?" That wasn't what he really wanted to ask.

"I'll be home Sunday afternoon." I gave him the information he really wanted. "Jean-Louis and I are flying from LaGuardia Sunday morning. I'll be in the house by four o'clock Sunday."

"Are you OK? Do you need any money? How's your hotel?"

"Dad, I'm just fine. Jean-Louis's father is putting us up at a house his company owns, and we're in hog heaven."

"Yes, Mr. Thibodeaux is a good man. You know, I've done some work for him over the years."

"No, sir, I didn't know that, but I'd sure like to hear about it when I get home."

"Well, remind me to tell you. With this medicine they have me on, sometimes I forget things."

"Yes, sir, I'll remind you."

"When does the competition start?" Now that he had established in his mind when I would be home, he could ask about the competition.

"We meet all the competitors tomorrow, and the actual competition is Thursday and Friday. Saturday there's an awards luncheon. Guess where it's at, Dad—the Waldorf. It's at the Waldorf-Astoria. I wonder if Mick is still the doorman."

I'm not sure how I did it, but I felt him smiling over the telephone. Good.

"Well, Dad, Jean-Louis and I are off for some dinner, and maybe we'll catch the early show at the Café Carlyle."

"Be careful. I love you." He hung up before I could respond. He didn't like good-byes at any time, and this leukemia thing was becoming one long good-bye.

I went downstairs, and, sure enough, Jean-Louis was stretched out in one of the leather club chairs with his shoes off and his feet toward the fireplace. He had a drink in his hand.

"Hey, Bubba," he said. "You know, if I wasn't so hungry for some jazz, we could just stay in tonight."

I was about to concur when he jumped up, slipped into his loafers, and said, "Let's go! It's three blocks to the Carlyle, and I want to get there before my feet freeze."

The food was average. Yankees just didn't seem to be able to get any pizazz into their food. Everything seemed to be built around meat and potatoes or some kind of steamed or broiled fish.

The piano playing, on the other hand, was *très* nice. The singer was a youngish brunette with cropped hair and a throaty voice that pulled you up toward the stage, especially when she dropped the volume and whispered into the microphone. Whew. I was in love. I told you I was easy, just not cheap.

I noticed Jean-Louis's hands moving across the tablecloth as if he were playing the song. Jean-Louis was a really good pianist, and he had a great voice as well. I wasn't bad on the ukulele, which I could make sound like a small guitar, but Jean-Louis—well, he was a virtuoso. Multi-talented, as it were.

We were actually back at the townhouse by ten. There was a requisite drink. Wasn't that the way the rich lived? They always had a drink after returning home and before going up to bed.

Everyone was in uniform. It seemed a little strange, but it was true. All the teams were wearing school blazers and gray trousers or skirts—well, skirt. There was only one woman in the competition. She was on the Southwest team, which was Stanford. She had a pleated gray-wool skirt and a haircut that said, "I'm hiding behind these bangs, and woe to the man who trespasses."

Jean-Louis and I stood apart from the others. Our blazers were a deep royal purple, and we were wearing charcoal trousers, not the lighter gray of all the others. The chevrons and fleurs-de-lis on our college badges gleamed in the strong lights of the room. Harvard and Stanford looked very much alike. It was hard to tell the difference between Cardinal and Crimson. Reed College, representing the Northwest, was also in reddish blazers. The maroon coats of Chicago weren't very far off the colors of the Indians or the Crimson, while Rice's blue blazers looked like your standard country-club issue. *Hmmm,* I thought. *Might create a little confusion in the minds of the judges, all these red blazers.*

We were introduced to a moderate-sized crowd in a small-ish auditorium in the Rockefeller Center. Harvard seemed to have brought a cheering section. We drew for order of speakers, and then we were led offstage to a waiting area where we couldn't hear the other speakers. The Stanford girl drew first. I was fourth, and Jean-Louis was seventh. Those were good spots because the judges wouldn't yet be too jaded or have heard the same material too many times. First was not good because of expectations. Last was not good because, well, it was last. The Stanford girl—I think her name was Janice—went off to be given the first topic and prepare her presentation. Ten minutes later the rather old-looking senior from Reed was called, then the Harvard guy in front of me.

They called me into a small room off the stage and hand-ed me a piece of paper. It read: "Your proposition is that the domino theory cannot be supported by evidence and thus cannot be used as an excuse to fight a war in Vietnam." Damn, damn, damn! I'd told Jean-Louis they were going to ask about Vietnam. I should have read those op-eds. Still, I thought I knew enough to make a good argument for this proposition. I did find it interesting that a semi-major college competition like this was taking such a political stand on an issue. I won-dered who was in charge.

Let's see. Rather than make it about the domino theory per se, I would make it about American Idealism gone awry. I would work the theory part in as an adjunct to emphasize that the whole world doesn't necessarily want or isn't able to use democracy. Don't attack the proposition directly; take it from an oblique angle. That was what Mr. Rush had taught me. I wondered if Jean-Louis would use the same strategy.

"So they do a cut down to three this evening. What happens if we're not in the top three? Do we go home? Do we need to make earlier travel arrangements?" I was talking with my mouth full of a Reuben sandwich. Well, not full exactly, but there was still enough in there to make me tilt my chin upward so it didn't come spilling out.

"Nope. We just take the day off and see New York. Besides, aren't we invited to the luncheon on Saturday?"

"Oh, yeah, I forgot. Everybody goes to the luncheon. I guess we'll get participation awards. Not half bad, though. A couple of freshmen taking on juniors and seniors. Hell, I bet that guy from Reed is in his thirties." I sounded petty, but I really didn't care. I was just making an observation.

"He is," Jean-Louis said. "While we were milling about in the ready room, he mentioned he had been in the army for several years and was only just now finishing up his degree."

I felt both mollified and a little guilty but not so much I couldn't enjoy the sandwich and Pepsi. No RC Colas in New York. None that I'd discovered, anyway.

"OK," Jean-Louis said over the hum of the crowd in front of the bulletin board. "They're posting the scores." He was caught up in the eddy of bodies. I didn't go over. I'd know soon enough, and really the experience had been a great one. The next day would be the top of the Empire State and the Met. I really wanted to see the Metropolitan Museum of Art.

Jean-Louis came over and sat on the bench next to me. His expression was almost one of disgust. "Damn! We almost got away with it. Just two points separating us from Harvard." He slapped me on the shoulder and grinned. "Well, I guess it's another early evening for us. Damn those Harvardians! Why didn't they perform better?" He rose and grabbed me by the shoulder of my blazer. "Come on, Bubba. We have to go home and read the op-eds."

"Where the hell is Spring Hill College?" Someone was yelling from the group in front of the board.

"I think Harvard is upset," Jean-Louis said.

"Where the hell is Spring Hill College?" It was a twenty-something, largish—as in Pillsbury Doughboy large—dark-haired individual wearing a Harvard blazer. He wasn't one of their competitors, so I could only guess he was a Harvard student or alum who was upset Harvard didn't make the final three.

Someone told him Spring Hill was in Mobile, and he immediately took great umbrage that a small school from the South had somehow toppled his mighty Crimson.

"Must have cheated," he said. "Only way they could make the top three is if they had the proposition in advance." He said this to the collected throng, most of whom were now watching his antics.

I was ready to move on, but Jean-Louis turned on a heel and upbraided the fellow for his spurious charge.

"Sir, I am from Spring Hill, and I find your fallacious proclamation injurious. Please apologize." Jean-Louis was using the thickest Cajun accent he could manage—which, believe me, was thick.

The Harvardian's jaw sagged somewhat, but he gathered himself. "Well, if you're one of the competitors, I know you must have cheated because there is no way any reasonable judge would not score you down for that incomprehensible accent." He said this in a Boston accent I'd heard only in movies.

"Shall I stand here awaiting some additional wise pearl from your lips so that I may accuse you of oxymoronic behavior, or are we to be treated only to words demonstrating affinity with the latter syllables of that adjective?" Jean-Louis had a tongue so keen that, when he chose, could flay three fillets from one flounder.

"What did you say?" The Harvardian acted as if he'd lost his place in a book.

"I think he called you a moron." Someone in the crowd helped him out.

"A moron? *A moron!* Oh, go away!" At this he used the back of his hand to indicate going away but in doing so did not calculate the distance Jean-Louis had closed on him. The backs of the tips of his fingers caught Jean-Louis just below the right cheek.

I was thinking Jean-Louis might just deck him, but he didn't. Instead he stepped backward one step, drew himself up, and announced, "I accept."

"What? *What?*" The man sounded like the class know-it-all who springs up for every question, trying to name the inventor of the steam engine before anyone else in class. "What do you mean, 'I accept'?"

Jean-Louis looked at me and grinned then faced his foe. "Well, first you accuse me of cheating. Then when I demand an apology, you challenge me. I accept that challenge. My card, sir. My seconds will be in touch. Who acts for you?" Jean-Louis whipped one of his calling cards from his pocket and proffered it to the Harvardian.

"Challenge you? I've no more challenged you than…what does he mean?" He turned to his fellow Harvard types. One, his accent placing him from below the Mason-Dixon, said, "Well, you did call him a cheat, and where we come from a slap on the face is a formal declaration of challenge." The Harvardian still looked confused. His fellow student explained, "He has accepted your offer to fight a duel."

"Duel? *A duel?* I never challenged anyone to a duel."

His colleague from the South again clarified the situation for him. "Well, it appears to all of us that you have given cause and challenge. If you back down now, he will have reason to declare you a coward. Not exactly the reputation you want to carry around your last year of college, is it? If you permit me, I understand these things, so I'll act on your behalf."

Stunned and still not sure what was happening, the Harvardian nodded his head as if to affirm acceptance of the offer.

I stepped forward and looked at Jean-Louis, who nodded to me. I took my card from my pocket and offered it to the Harvard southerner.

"Jean Anton Jourdain. I have the honor, sir, to act on behalf of Mr. Thibodeaux."

My respondent took the card, held out his hand, and said, "I'm afraid we don't carry cards at Harvard. I am William Jefferson Benton of Virginia, and I act on behalf of Mr. Peabody." He pronounced it *peebadee*.

I shook his hand, but as I did, Peabody suddenly came to life.

"Duel? *Duel?* Not me. I'll not be part of some brutal, provincial southern tradition. No one at Harvard will hold me accountable for not fighting a duel."

Benton took him by the elbow and said, "Winston, the majority of these people aren't from Harvard. They now know your name, your school, and from your accent that you're a native Bostonian. How long do you think it will be before this story makes the rounds of the Ivy League? No, I'm afraid you'll have to respond, especially since you gave offense dressed in a Harvard blazer. And you can't call dueling a southern tradition...the first duel in America was fought at Plymouth Rock in 1621."

Seeing this as my opportunity, I stepped in. "As the challenged, Mister Thibodeaux has the choice of venue and weapons. May I suggest Central Park between the skating rink and the zoo at eight tomorrow morning?" Benton nodded in assent.

"Weapons." I stopped here and mused a bit. "Weapons… yes. Weapons will be snowballs at ten paces."

The crowd laughed. People start repeating, "Snowballs. They're going to duel with snowballs!"

I leaned in, taking Benton by the lapel. Pulling him closer, I whispered, "I feel it only fair to inform you that my principal was, just last year, offered a contract by the Los Angeles Dodgers. He throws almost any ball well in excess of eighty miles an hour with the accuracy of Don Drysdale. At ten paces he will put your principal in the hospital, even with a snowball. But if your principal were to publicly apologize before we adjourn this evening, I'm sure it would be acceptable."

Benton looked me in the eye and said, "No lie?"

"I swear." I could be no clearer.

Benton grabbed Peabody and hauled him into a corner. There was a bit of gesticulating on Peabody's part, but within a minute they were back. The crowd was still gathered. Snowballs were still being discussed.

"On the advice of counsel," Peabody said sheepishly, "I must say that perhaps I was too caught up in the sadness of our team not advancing in the competition, and my judgment of the Spring Hill team was incorrect. I apologize and assure you I offered no challenge to you."

Jean-Louis again drew himself to attention, captured Peabody with his intense, inescapable emerald stare, and announced, "I accept, and I apologize for referring to your behavior as oxymoronic. I fault myself for dealing in half truths." But then he reached down and took Peabody's hand and pumped it three times while grabbing Peabody's elbow with his left hand and pulling him in closer.

The crowd cheered at the show of good sportsmanship. Jean-Louis had conquered another small world. His was the story that would make its way through the Ivy League. His offer to fight a duel would sweep like wildfire through the all-male colleges of the North and the South. Not out of his freshmen year and already he had a national reputation.

The second day was anticlimactic. The subject was economics— not my strongest area, but Jean-Louis and I managed to place second after Chicago. Stanford, with the only female competitor, took third. I looked for Mick at the Waldorf, but he wasn't there on Saturdays, they told me. He was still the head doorman, but he didn't work weekends. Too bad. I would have liked very much to visit with him. Perhaps I would return to New York in the not-so-distant future, but for the moment I was concerned with getting home.

The airplane was four hours late. We arrived Sunday evening instead of in the afternoon. As I walked into the terminal from the tarmac, I saw my father seated in one of the waiting-area chairs. He looked weak, but he smiled. I leaned down to kiss his forehead. Again he smelled of sickness.

"Four hours," my mother said. "He's been sitting here for four hours. Wouldn't go home. He was afraid the airplane would arrive before he could get back. I don't know how he did it."

I helped my father up so he could lean on me for the walk to the car. I would have gotten a wheelchair, but my father would not be seen in public in a wheelchair. We walked slowly. I recounted the duel story to him. He laughed—like really laughed. He enjoyed the story.

Jean-Louis caught up with us, having stopped to give his phone number to one of the stewardesses on the flight. "I suppose Jack is filling you full of stories he invented while sleeping during the presentations."

"Yes," my father replied, "I suppose he is. But you should be careful, Jean-Louis. You should do more research on individuals before you provoke them. One of these days, that empathic mesmerism might well fail you. You always need an escape route."

"You are correct, *mon maître*, but I have my escape route. You know him well. His name is Jack."

We had reached the car. Jean-Louis helped my father in while I put my mother in the backseat. As he rounded the driver's side to leave, he leaned in to me and whispered, "You're so lucky to have such a wise father."

I tapped him lightly. "I know."

June 1966

CHAPTER 9

SWITCHING TRACKS

I SIGNED THE HONOR PLEDGE, put the cap back on my pen, and looked out the window. The rain showers had passed, and the afternoon sun's rays refracted to form a rainbow in the foreground of the gun-gray cotton clouds fleeing toward the eastern horizon. Taking up my exam bluebooks, I walked to the front of the classroom and deposited them with those of other students on the professor's desk. There were still several students struggling with one or more of the questions on the European history final. I wondered which of the five questions was giving them the most difficulty. Probably the one about who Queen Victoria liked best, Gladstone or Disraeli.

Does it really matter? I asked myself. *Why do I need to know which prime minister a nineteenth-century English queen preferred?* Then, remembering what Mr. Rush had explained more than once, I recalled that although the question might not matter, it was important that I be able to use whatever relevant facts I knew to craft an argument that arrived at a well-reasoned answer. The question was as much about logical thinking and rhetoric as it was about European history. A lot like the questions at the rhetorical speaking contest in New York.

Satisfied with this answer, I slung my book bag over my shoulder and headed for my car. As always the storm had left the air clean, even though the gutters ran yellow with pine pollen. The humidity remained high, but that was nothing new. Mobile always had high humidity levels.

Also expected were the puddles on the seats of my 1949 Willys Jeepster convertible. The last true phaeton automobile made in America, its side curtains simply could not keep the weather out, especially when the rain was wind driven. I was used to this and kept multiple chamois cloths in an old ammo can under the backseat.

"Why don't you get a decent car?" Jean-Louis appeared as if from nowhere, reached over the back of the seat, and took another chamois cloth out of the can. Standing on the steel step on the side of the rear wheel well, he began wiping water off the backseat.

"I don't hear you complaining when we take it out on the beach at Gulf Shores." I said. Jean-Louis and I enjoyed the Jeepster's four-wheel drive. We often roared up and down the deserted beach, throwing up rooster tails of water as the car raced through the remnants of retreating waves on the hard sand. And race it would, for Uncle Gale had replaced the original anemic, four-cylinder engine with a Pontiac six cylinder. There wasn't, however, anything to be done about keeping the rain out of a car that didn't have windows and depended on plastic curtains that rolled down from its convertible top.

"Sure, that's great, but you're grown up. You got this thing to haul around cleaning supplies for your toilet-cleaning business, but you're out of that now—so you should get something more befitting a...what exactly does my father have you doing?" Jean-Louis's voice was muffled as he leaned down between the front and rear seats to sop up a puddle on the floor mat.

"Investigative accounting. My father is teaching me some of his techniques for spotting discrepancies and figuring out whether they're due to sloppy accounting or to someone trying to hide something. Your dad has me going over accounting from his various, shall we say, enterprises. I have to say it's more interesting than I'd thought it would be. You have to know about the details of the business to understand the costs, profits, reinvestments, and so forth. And working with my father has given me a totally new perspective on how much of a math genius he truly is. He has all these great ideas, some of which involve visualization and pattern seeking. It's fascinating. By the way, I'm looking real close at that air freight company you're working for."

"So you're following in your father's footsteps, but you still intend to major in languages and theology. Why not business or accounting?" Jean-Louis held the chamois out over the parking lot and twisted it tightly. At least a pint of water fell onto the already wet blacktop. Then he shook the cloth by its corners to dry it. This, of course, was a futile gesture given the humidity. Leaning over the backseat of the Jeepster again, he dragged the cloth across the vinyl seat covering.

"Hey, how much did you pay for this thing?" His voice was half lost under the seat.

"Three hundred and fifty dollars, and that's with the replaced engine. It was a great deal since I know it must have cost Uncle Gale at least half that much just to put in the Pontiac engine."

I busied myself trying to get the driver's seat as dry as possible, so I wouldn't have to sit in a puddle and get my khakis wet. After two more swipes, I returned to Jean-Louis's earlier question.

"I don't study accounting for the same reason you aren't going to major in engineering or math. All you talk about is flying jets, but you've made the same decision I have, and I suspect it has more than a little to do with our mutual tutor. We're studying the humanities because we hope it will make us better thinkers. Or maybe it's because we want to understand people and the world better, and the humanities are the path to a better understanding. Or maybe it's just because we're contrary and don't always do the smart thing. At least that would be the answer in your case." I smiled.

Although I thought the seat was dry enough, I took another chamois cloth from the can and spread it where I would sit behind the wheel. As I leaned over the backseat, I heard a pop as Jean-Louis snapped a wet chamois in my direction. It stung a little, but my wallet took the majority of the contact.

Maybe it is time to get another car, I thought. I made a mental note to talk to Uncle Gale about something more modern. Maybe this time something with windows.

Better yet, I thought, *I've got enough time to go by Uncle Gale's office right now and still make it by the client's office to pick up his documents to review with Dad later in the evening.*

Looking at Jean-Louis, I announced, "Dang it, when you're right, you're right. Want to go over to Uncle Gale's and see what he can piece together for me?"

"Can't. Got a flight up to Montgomery this afternoon, and I want to get up and back before it's too dark." Jean-Louis put the chamois back in a second ammo box that I kept for the wet cloths. Unfortunately I hadn't dried the cloths since the last rain, and the can emitted a notably rancid smell the minute he opened it.

"Phew! Man, do something so you don't have to carry this can around," Jean-Louis said, recoiling backward and slamming the lid on the ammo can. "See ya." He walked off toward his car, a '57 Chevy Bel-Air convertible that had a metallic copper paint job. It was a beauty—nine years old and already a classic. Jean-Louis knew how to pick 'em. Or, in this case, Mr. Thibodeaux had known because this '57 had been Jean-Louis's father's when it was new.

Turning so I could see Jean-Louis's back as he walked off, I yelled, "How you gonna fly jets if you're afraid to fly in the dark?"

Without looking back Jean-Louis raised his left hand, gave me the universal salute of disgust, and then laughed.

I guessed Uncle Gale was in his office at the back of the main garage as I pulled my Willys into a customer parking spot. Acknowledging the mechanics as I walked through the garage, I stopped long enough to schmooze the secretary, Louise, and then knocked and entered the office. As usual my pseudo-uncle in fact but real uncle in practice was poring over numerous papers: parts orders, invoices, tax statements, and all the other wood-pulp-based paraphernalia businesses require to stay open.

"I know you have a business office," I said. "Why on Earth do you go over all these invoices and tax receipts yourself?"

Uncle Gale looked up and smiled. "Nice to see you, too, Boy."

There it was again—that old family name. Nobody outside the family called me Boy anymore, and even my mother had taken to calling me Jack.

"You know, Uncle Gale, now that I'm nineteen and all, maybe you could call me Jack."

Uncle Gale looked quizzical for a moment and then replied, "Sure thing, Boy. Jack it is."

I rolled my eyes to the ceiling and, moving a pile of car titles from a chair, sat down.

"Sure, you're all grown up now," he continued. "You're in college. You don't clean toilets anymore, you're dating some pretty college coeds, and you think that means the family is going to somehow stop seeing you as the Boy." Uncle Gale looked serious. "There are just some things that don't change, and they don't change because people don't want them to change. There's comfort in tradition. You just don't know it yet, and it isn't something you're going to learn in college. So how about this? When there's somebody not family around, I'll call you Jack, but if it's just family, I'll call you Boy."

Knowing I was on the losing side of the argument, I rolled my eyes again, sighed, and accepted the compromise with a nod.

However, I realized Uncle Gale had given me my opening, so I sortied, "Speaking of tradition and comfort and being out of the toilet-cleaning business, I was thinking it might be time to consider a car that keeps the weather out a little better than my Willys. Not that I don't like the Jeepster, but Jean-Louis reminded me today that if I have to go to clients' offices to pick up accounting documents, I probably should drive something a little more non-toilet-cleaning-business-like."

Uncle Gale leaned back in his swivel chair. "And what did you have in mind?"

I thought for a moment. "Something newer but not new. I can't afford a new car, plus I'd rather have something the bugs have been worked out of, and you know Dad doesn't really believe in new anythings. I'm thinking something that I won't have to wipe the seats down after every passing thunderstorm. Perhaps something that looks, well, maybe just a little sporty. In other words no big Buicks or four-door Chevys. Maybe a coupe."

Uncle Gale looked pensive. I waited for his response.

"I've got a '59 MGA out back. It's red," he said.

As much as I would have liked to tool around town in a little MG sports car, it wasn't what I really had in mind. "No, I think I need a backseat and something a little higher, so I don't drag my elbow on the ground when I make left turns."

Uncle Gale chuckled, and I hoped he was thinking, *The kid is growing up. How many nineteen-year-olds would pass up a sports car?* He looked at me. "So that means Corvettes and Thunderbirds are out, although the Thunderbirds have gotten so big these days—they fall more into the two-door Buick LeSabre category than the Corvette. How about a Thunderbird?"

I did not and never have liked the Thunderbird from its inception, so I had no problem resisting the thought. "No, Uncle Gale. I think a Thunderbird is a little too rich for my pocketbook. Speaking of which, are you willing to carry a loan if I don't have enough cash?"

Looking almost hurt, my uncle replied, "Let's find you something before we talk about money. Although I think I may have just the thing. The owner thought it was too small for what he needed and traded it for a '65 Galaxy four-door. We just went over it mechanically and replaced the two-barrel carb with a rebuilt Holley four barrel. It's in really good shape and would make a great car for you."

As he said this, he picked up a manila folder from among the score or more on his desk. He moved from behind the desk, through the door, and out toward the back of the shop. I walked with him. In the rear right corner of the first garage bay sat a

1963 Ford Falcon Sprint convertible. The top was white, and the body was turquoise, a color popular on Thunderbirds. It was a pretty car. It sat next to a 1964 four-door Chevy Impala, which only accentuated the Falcon's smaller size.

Like the top, the inside of the car was white with two seats separated by a small silver console box in the front and the standard bench in the back. A four-speed floor shifter was mounted just in front of a pack of gauges that provided the water and oil temperatures. An ammeter and a manifold pressure gauge were mounted there as well. A tachometer was centered at the top center of the dash. Under the dash was a long, narrow box with vents.

"Now, that's a real oxymoron," I said, thinking back to Jean-Louis's encounter with the Harvardian in New York.

"An oxy what?" Uncle Gale asked.

"Oxymoron. A compact paradox. In this case air conditioning in a convertible."

"Not a pair of dox or even a single dox," Uncle Gale parried. "In our summer humidity, you'll be glad to arrive at your client's without that sweat-stained shirt you get in an un-air-conditioned car." Uncle Gale's puns weren't as sharp as my father's; nonetheless, it was a good play.

I glanced quickly at the sweat stains under the arms of my blue oxford cloth shirt and silently agreed air conditioning might not be a bad thing.

The test drive convinced me Uncle Gale was right. It was the perfect car for me. As I started to pull it back into the garage bay, Uncle Gale issued directions. "Just park it there next to the Jeepster."

As I turned off the ignition, I asked, "How much?"

"Well, it cost three thousand new, and it's only got eighteen thousand miles on it. New carb and new whitewalls. I reckon I could get two for it on one of the lots. So yeah, two thousand."

I gulped visibly. Going from a three-hundred-dollar car to a two-thousand-dollar car was, for me, like leaping the Grand Canyon on a bicycle. In a word: impossible.

"Oh, well." I sighed. "It was fun during the test drive to imagine Misses Amanda, Belle, and Courtney—or maybe even Miss Anne Marie—their hair blowing in the wind, as we headed down the highway to Dauphin Island."

"So, too much?" Uncle Gale asked.

"As in way too much. I'm not making all that much working part time because I'm on a baseball scholarship, and some of the time in the late winter and all through the spring is taken up playing baseball. I was thinking that if I could make enough, I might drop the scholarship and work more, but that would take a lot of money and some loans. So yes, two thousand is way too much."

"How about three to four hundred?" Uncle Gale smiled as he asked.

"I'm not a charity case, Uncle Gale, and you're not giving me a car. Dad would never let me accept it."

"Look, Boy," said Uncle Gale as he put on his serious face. "It's not charity; it's business. In this folder I have an agreement that says you will, when asked, review the financial records of any and all of my shops and lots. For that you'll be paid a per task wage, but to ensure I have your services, the agreement further stipulates that you will receive a two-thousand-dollar-per-year retainer. So you have to declare the two thousand as income and pay the tax on it. You also have to pay the tags and license fees for the car. I figure your state and federal income tax and license will cost you about three hundred dollars. So do you want the car or not? And are you willing to undertake periodic reviews of my financials?"

"Of course I want the car, and yes, I'd love to be on your payroll, but I'm too young and don't have the experience to do what you need done. You already have my father, so why do you need me?" I felt I had to be honest. This was, after all, family.

"Jack, let's don't talk about your father right now. It makes me cry just to think about it. Suffice it to say he isn't going to be able to work much longer, and I trust you, as family, more than I would trust some firm of accountants who are looking to bill me top dollar. You're going to do just fine." He held out the contract and fished in his pocket protector for a pen.

"And oh yeah, I'll give you two-fifty for the Jeepster. If I put it up on blocks for five years or so, it's going to become a classic, and I'll get some serious money for it. Either that or I'll paint it red, put some new seats in it, and sell it next month over at Pensacola as a humdinger of a beach car."

It took only thirty minutes to do the paperwork and call Lawrence, the State Farm rep, about changing insurance. The Falcon insurance cost half again more than the Jeepster's, but I was happy to pay. As I signed over the Willys title, I stood up from the desk and remarked, "Wow, some things are just meant to be. I mean, what are the odds somebody would trade in the Falcon just before I decided I needed a new car? I mean, what are the odds?"

As I pulled out of the parking lot, Louise asked Uncle Gale, "What did he mean that someone would trade the Falcon just before he decided he needed a new car? You've had that car in the shop for at least three months. In fact, you've turned down four offers on it."

Uncle Gale looked highly amused as he placed a finger to his lips to indicate silence. "I know that, you know that, and Jack's father knows that, but Jack doesn't, and that's the way it's going to stay. Right?"

Louise couldn't stop a smile spreading across her face. "Right you are, Boss." She didn't stop chuckling all the way back to her desk. She would eventually tell me the story.

Twenty minutes later I pulled the Falcon into an angled parking space in front of the client's office. Emerging from the car I glanced quickly at my underarms. Completely dry. I looked almost professional.

"I expected you earlier." My father's voice sounded weak rising from within the ever-growing teak lounge chair.

"Yes, sir. I intended to be home earlier, but I got caught up at Uncle Gale's. I thought I needed a new car, and—well, I have a new car, but I can take it back if you think I should."

I was concerned my father might not approve of the deal. After all I was only nineteen and could in no way conduct a full audit by myself. My father might think I was taking money under false pretenses.

Slowly making his way to the front door and onto the porch, my father considered the Falcon. He leaned against one of the white pillars as he looked at the car I'd parked at the curb in front of the house. The heavy, late afternoon air was perfumed by jasmine and early blooming gardenias that grew along the sides of the porch and over the picket fence that separated the house from the side yard.

"Looks like a solid piece of iron, apart from that ragtop. How does it handle?"

"Nicely. Not like a sports car, but better than that big Buick of yours." I smiled as I realized my father thought the car was OK. But then I had to tell him about the agreement with Uncle Gale. My father reached for the arm of one of the wicker rocking chairs and lowered himself gently at first, but, as his weight shifted, the movement ended with an "umphh!" signaling a semi-controlled collapse.

I pulled a rocker over catty-cornered to my father's. As I rocked, slowly I began the story of my afternoon's adventure. My father rocked also, almost in cadence with me, and listened.

As I finished I leaned forward in the rocker, hands clasped under my chin, elbows on my knees.

"And so here we are. I have a new car, a new sort of job, and maybe a life direction I had no idea existed a year ago." I rose and reentered the living room, where I poured my father two fingers of bourbon and myself a small scotch. I put three times as much soda in the glass as scotch. I took the glasses out to the porch. The screen door slammed behind me, its spring twanging like the lingering last note of a banjo solo.

Back in my rocker, glass in hand, I continued, "I don't know, Dad. This all seems so right, yet it doesn't seem right at all. I seem to be so…blessed." I caught myself, for I had almost said *lucky*, and once again my father would have wondered if I was a dunderhead because we both knew that luck was something you created for yourself by being prepared for opportunity—and sometimes, just sometimes, doing things that might help create an opportunity.

My father sipped the bourbon, holding the glass in his fingertips, viewing me through the facets on its sides. "Jack, at the moment I can see three of you, one distinctly and two almost as well. One to the right and one to the left. So, right now, are there three of you or just one?"

I considered the question. "Just one."

My father looked as if he was about to comment but reconsidered and asked, "Let's say you meet three other people at the same time. Are there three of you or just one?"

After thinking about his question, I replied, "I suppose each person seeing me through different eyes would make three of me."

"Would it?" my father asked. "Only three?"

Once more I thought before answering, "Oh! Of course. There's the way I see myself, so it would be four."

"Just four? What about how you see your relationship with each individual and the three collectively as a group?"

I did the math quickly. "Eight? Eight of me?"

"Eight is a good enough number. Now, of those eight, which viewpoint is the most important?"

I started to say, "Depends upon the situation," but as I got the *de* out of my mouth, I caught the look in my father's eyes and tentatively asked, "Mine?"

"Yes," my father replied, "yours." He sipped his bourbon. "You are nineteen. You are a legal adult. You may sign contracts, execute agreements, and do anything else that an adult is entitled to do. You do not need my blessing to undertake anything you want to do. I have faith that if you believe it is the correct and right thing to do, then you should do it. You and your uncle Gale reached an agreement. That's all there is to it."

I listened and then countered, "But Dad, I'm a complete tyro in this area. I'm afraid I'll let Uncle Gale down if I have to do something without your help. He goes on about trusting family more than anyone else, and I'm worried I might let him down."

My father looked impressed that I used the word *tyro*, but then, out of nowhere, he asked, "Jack, are you reconciled with your decision not to go to West Point?"

"Reconciled? What exactly does that mean? If it means am I happy then the answer is that I'm content, for I didn't expect to achieve happiness from West Point...or did I?" Here I stopped and searched inside my own mind for what I had expected from West Point.

My father sipped more bourbon and let the silence expand. He listened to a mockingbird harassing a crow in the large oak tree. Farther up the tree, a red-bellied woodpecker busied himself picking at the segmented bark where caterpillars had hidden their cocoons, now doomed to become their coffins. My father settled himself farther into the fan-backed wicker chair that had become so large it almost swallowed him. There had been a day, which now seemed several lifetimes ago, when the chair had barely fit his frame. But now…

Finally I broke the silence and said, "I think perhaps what I expected from West Point was to be part of the brotherhood of arms. To belong to something larger than myself and to dedicate myself with my brothers-in-arms to the mission of that vocation."

My father rocked and listened. Then he said, "Yes, I suspected as much when you began talking about the academy when you were five. Still, consider this. There are many brotherhoods. The police have a brotherhood, firemen, and others as well. Not all are for the good, and just as individuals do not always see the 'right thing' as others do, so too is it with brotherhoods."

He paused and then continued, "The Jesuits will be after you. You're exactly the type of young man they want in their ranks. The soldiers of Christ. As you demonstrate your leadership abilities, other organizations may reach out to you. I have faith you will make the decision that is best for you and the family."

I sipped at the scotch-flavored soda in my glass. "So Uncle Gale is right. Family is a kind of brotherhood, isn't it?"

"Yes, Jack, your Uncle Gale is right. Of course, he meant your de facto family and not just your blood family. You are already part of a brotherhood, and whether you feel yourself ready or not, you've already begun to accept a leadership position in that brotherhood.

"This is a discussion we will continue, but we've cut into work time long enough. Let's get at those ledgers you brought home. I have a suspicion someone in one of the branch offices of this firm is sailing a bit too close to the wind. Let's see if my hunch proves correct."

My father's voice became stronger when he spoke of numbers and patterns.

When my mother arrived home, out of the corner of my eye I saw her slide the back door shut and stand outside the kitchen. My father and I were at the kitchen table. With our two heads of dark, wavy hair pressed very much together, my father said, "See, this figure repeats a monthly expense, but it shouldn't always be the same as it is because it's a variable services expenditure based on a progressive rate for printing reproductions. In this business such requirements should vary from month to month, but they don't. We have to dig deeper. We need to start thinking like a crook. How would we rob our boss if this job was ours?" Once again my father was teaching me how to think critically.

From the corner of my eye, I could see my mother smiling.

June 1967

CHAPTER 10

THE END OF
THE BEGINNING

HE FELL INTO A COMA on the first of June. He had made it
from the chair to the couch, where he lay as I came through the
door with clients' ledgers in my book bag.

I called for an ambulance, which arrived almost half an
hour later. During that time, I knelt on one knee and held my
father's hand. At one point his eyes fluttered, and I, with great
hope, looked into them. Locking my green eyes with his dark-
brown ones, he said, "Jack, everything is going to be fine. I
want you to know there is a God." Then his eyes fluttered once
more and closed.

After helping to lift him into the back of the ambulance, I
insisted on riding next to him. The emergency vehicle moved
slowly through the heavy going-home traffic between the ship-
yard and Brookley Air Force Base. Still holding my father's
hand, I closely watched his eyes, and once again they fluttered,
opened, and focused on me.

I looked into the depths of his eyes and saw that my father was fully there. "It's OK, Dad," I said. "Everything is going to be fine." His eyes moved in recognition of the reassurance and then closed once more. They never opened again. He lingered until the sixth of June and died as I held one hand and my mother, his wife, held the other.

In death my father reverted to the Catholicism from whence he had come. The archbishop's office sent a note of condolence to my mother. Saint Matthew's Catholic Church was filled with mourners, and a few notables showed up. Mr. Thibodeaux was there with his family. A city councilman who owned a car dealership and some service stations attended the service. There were lots of small businessmen, bakers, bicycle-shop owners, jewelers, restaurant managers, and bar owners and managers. Strangely, the wives of several prominent Mobilians attended. All wore black and sat in the back of the church. The single largest contingent, though, was the battalion of the soldiers of Jesus in their black cassocks. They considered my father one of their greatest recruiting failures, and they wanted others to acknowledge that while he might not have worn the collar, Anton Jourdain's soul was that of a Jesuit.

The section of pews reserved for family overflowed with the de facto family of which my father was so proud. The church reverberated as Kent Rush delivered the eulogy in his practiced baritone.

The choir from the orphanage sang during the memorial service. A solo tenor sang "Danny Boy," and then, accompanied by the boys' choir, sang *"Non Nobis Domine."*

He was buried in our family plot so near Spring Hill College that I could easily walk over to visit his grave between my classes.

As I think back on that day, I find it strange that my last words to my father were essentially the same last words my father spoke to me. "Everything is going to be fine..."

Now that I knew God really did exist, I could be very angry with him. And I was for quite some time.

February 1969

CHAPTER 11

TRAVELING ON

SLEEP EVADED ME. SOMETHING WAS poking me in my hip, but I was too exhausted to get up and search my trouser pockets for whatever it was. Maybe I wasn't exactly exhausted—even though I had danced all the previous evening—but was instead suffering after-effects from the evening's champagne or brandy. I had certainly consumed some quantities of both. Not just any champagne but ice-cold, really brut Taittinger. Jean-Louis's father had it specially iced for the ball. Nothing better than ice-cold, brut Taittinger. The brandy hadn't been French but something produced from peaches, illicitly and in small quantities, by a family in Mississippi. It had been very expensive and very good. You had to be somebody to get it, and Jean-Louis's father was somebody.

Sheer willpower eventually enabled me to stand by my bed and, in the dark, try to take my boots off. They resisted. I sat down on the edge of the bed and tried harder, but they still resisted. It was as if they were held in place by some invisible force. Giving up, I took my trousers off. Getting them off over my boots took some doing. The trouser legs were tapered. The wool was heavy and had been hot in the ballroom. As I tugged the trousers over the boots, I realized why I couldn't get the boots off. The trousers were held straight in the crease by stirrups under the arch of each boot. It was, after all, a uniform—the uniform of one of Mobile's more interesting mystic societies.

After fighting with the trousers, the boots were easy. I flipped them off heel to toe. Taking up the trousers, I tried to search the pockets for what had been gouging me in the hip. Unable to find any pockets, I finally reached for my bedside lamp. It took what seemed minutes to adjust my eyes so I could see other images that weren't blurred. When I did, I discovered the trousers had no pockets. I decided the discomfort in my hip must have come from a button on my uniform jacket, which I had thrown on the bed before collapsing on top of it.

"Is this my last Mardi Gras?" Unexpectedly, the real reason I couldn't sleep revealed itself. "My last Mardi Gras?"

"It doesn't have to be," I replied to myself. "I can go to law school in New Orleans and have Mardi Gras there and then come back to Mobile to practice law." Still, the thought of law school made me nauseous. "Is that what I really want to do? Be a lawyer?" I sat on the edge of the bed, half awake, half asleep—or so it seemed, until light began to show through the louvers of the plantation shutters over my bedroom windows.

I found my way to the bathroom and stood under the shower for a long time. The hot water didn't revive me, so I turned the hot-water faucet off and stood under the cold water as long as I could tolerate it. It had the desired effect. My brain cleared, and I felt almost as if the day and night before had never happened. But they had, and now I was faced with decisions I would rather not make.

I found my mother already in the kitchen. The pot of coffee on the stove was steaming. I poured some into my mug and sat at the large table in the middle of the room that, for the past two years, had seemed empty with only two people there.

"Did you enjoy the ball?" my mother asked, almost as if she expected me to say that I had not enjoyed escorting one of the princesses of the court and, perhaps, the most beautiful girl in Mobile. She could still read me like a Dick and Jane reader.

"Oh yes, ma'am, I had a great time. You should have come." She had been invited but had declined. She had always enjoyed Mardi Gras balls, but since my father died, she was less likely to socialize, especially at events where an escort was expected and dancing was on the agenda.

"Did you dance all the waltzes with Anne Marie?" My mother was fishing now.

"No, ma'am, not all of them."

"Most of them?" She was going to bracket me until she hit the target.

"I didn't really keep count, Mom."

"Well, did she dance with anyone else more than once?"

"Not that I noticed."

"So she danced most of the waltzes with you?" She had me.

"Yes, ma'am, I suppose so."

"And you're seeing her again tonight?"

"Ah yes, ma'am, that's the plan."

"Don't you have college work to finish up?"

"No, ma'am, we're off this week. I have my comprehensives to study for, but you seem to forget I'm not taking any hard courses this semester. I already have more than enough quality credits and semester hours to graduate. If I had wanted, I could have tried my comps in December and graduated in January, assuming, of course, I passed the comps."

"So let me get this straight," she continued. "After four years of college and God knows how many courses, projects, internships, and papers, you still have to pass a *comprehensive* exam in order to graduate?"

"Only in my major subject area. But since I'm majoring in more than one subject, I have to pass comps in each of the areas. So I have modern languages and theology. The latter includes an exam in ancient Hebrew, Greek and Latin plus Bible, dogma, comparative religions, and history of the church.

"In modern languages I have tests in Italian, French, Spanish, and Arabic. The spoken tests will be easiest. The written tests are all about grammar and such, including translating some fairly difficult passages from various classical and modern texts, so I expect them to be harder. I'm spending this semester taking Physical Education, Teaching Shooting Sports, and Aviation Skills. They're all lab courses, so that's the twelve hours I need to be a full-time student to stay out of the draft. The free time I've generated, I use to study for comps in my major areas of concentration."

"Oh" was all my overwhelmed mother could muster as a response.

"I'm studying with Jean-Louis, of course, since we're majoring in the same areas. I'll be getting together with him this afternoon. Then we'll be going to a Mardi Gras party at the Café Royale and then the parade. So I'll be late again but not as late as last night."

"You mean, not as late as this morning," my mother corrected me.

"Yes, ma'am, not as late as this morning."

I sipped at my coffee, blowing away the steam before each sip. I held the mug in two hands with just the tips of my fingers. I looked over the rim at my mother. "I sure miss Dad. He'd know what I should do."

"I don't think you mean it quite that way," my mother answered. "Your father almost never told you what to do. He helped you decide what you wanted to do or, in some cases, what you needed to do. But he never told you what to do."

"Yes, ma'am, I understand that, but I guess what I meant was that I miss the interaction where I could sit down, have a discussion, and walk away feeling I was making the right decision. I suppose Dad validated my decisions."

"I suppose…" My mother turned away, tears forming in her eyes. "I suppose…that's as good a way of describing it as any other." She dabbed at her eyes with the brightly colored Mardi Gras napkin that our maid, Dora, had put at her place at the table. The napkin was a deep purple with a green-and-gold harlequin stitched on it. Dora was a whiz with embroidery. Purple, green, and gold were the traditional colors of Mardi Gras, and they were everywhere during February. This was a difficult time of year for my mother. She had met my father at a Mardi Gras soirée the year after the war. They had married that fall, and Mardi Gras was always a special time for them. He loved to dance, and the balls were perfect opportunities to show off his abilities. She played Ginger Rogers, danced backward, twirled on occasion, and smiled.

Now, with semidry eyes, she smiled a little at the memory of his rhumba moves. It was ironic that since he was half Choctaw, he wasn't welcome at the all-white clubs, but everyone invited him to their Mardi Gras parties. It was the perplexing mix of blood and attitudes of the Deep South. "Good to see ya, wouldn't wanna be ya." But in some cases, they would want to be you. Or, perhaps, just to be with you. My mother knew any number of women who had lusted after her husband. Most of them were lily-white wives of prominent husbands. Almost all of them were former debutantes. Some of them were, in truth, more scarlet than white, but as was said in Mobile, "rich daddies and husbands can buy lots of hush."

Now my mother saw me being pursued by at least three daughters of those same lily-white debs, including a wild child whose dress was already a pale shade of pink. I think she wondered how much of my popularity was because of my brother-like relationship with Jean-Louis Thibodeaux and how much of it would have happened naturally. It really didn't matter. The Thibodeaux family had been a godsend as far as she was concerned. When my father died, they were there, and if not for them, she thought I would have struggled with the loss of my father much more than I did. She was right.

Eyes still glistening a little, my mother turned back to face me. "So what are your options?" She wasn't my father, but she understood me in her own way.

"Of course, there's the army. I could go to Officer Candidate School and become an officer. I mean, OCS isn't West Point, but it will give me a commission if I go there." I paused for both of us to remember how I had turned down the appointment to the academy to stay at home because my father was dying of leukemia.

"Then there's grad school or law school." I paused a minute to sip the coffee, rose from the table, and went to the stove to top off and warm my mug from the pot.

"I actually thought a great deal about seminary. Everyone thinks I would make a great priest, but I find I like women far too much to even contemplate the priesthood. Besides, while I have this passion for doing the right thing, I don't think the strictures of the church necessarily allow the right thing to happen all the time. I guess I'm like Dad in that when he met you, all thoughts of becoming a Jesuit flew out of his mind."

My mother's jaw tightened. She tried to bite her tongue but had to ask, "So you think you've found Miss Right?"

"Oh no, ma'am, nothing like that. All the girls I've dated are nice enough, but they want something different from what I want. They want big weddings, two children, country clubs, and husbands who make a lot of money. It sounds shallow, but it isn't, not really, because that's how they've been raised. I just know I like being around women far too much to consider taking vows that involve forgoing carnal pleasure." I looked over my mug at her, chuckled just a little, and sipped at the now again-steaming mug. I thought she might blush, but she didn't.

"But that isn't what I want," I continued.

My mother relaxed, no doubt thinking, *Thank God he hasn't fallen for that Anne Marie.*

"Mr. Rush and Mr. Thibodeaux have been talking to me about working in the *societé*, as an assistant to Mr. Thibodeaux," I said. "Normally that would be something Jean-Louis would do, but he wants to fly jets, so he's off to the air force. Interestingly, Mr. Rush says that if I go to work for Mr. Thibodeaux, the draft board won't bother me. I don't know how that can be, but Mr. Rush has never been wrong. He's going to take me to dinner next week at the Café Royale. He says he has something important to share with me."

My mother didn't answer immediately, preferring to let me think a moment. She was glad Kent Rush was helping out. She thought that as mentor to both Jean-Louis and me, he had been instrumental in molding us into the intelligent, caring young men she believed we had become. Still, she knew neither Mr. Rush nor Mr. Thibodeaux was my father. She believed I missed my father more than I admitted. She thought about what my father might say in this situation.

Finally she said, "Jack, do you remember when you and your father got on that train thing? Do you remember how he taught you about the relationship between reality and imagination? About visualizing? Then, when you were older, how the two of you talked about recognizing the right thing and how you began gaining confidence in your ability to rely on yourself and make your own decisions? How using that formula you made the decision to forgo West Point? How your talks with him helped crystallize those important things in your mind? What I think you need now is to talk to your father."

I looked at my mother again, with just my eyes over the top of the mug. The rising steam formed a foreground that gave the picture a mystical quality.

"Yes, ma'am, I think you're right."

My mother went off to her job as a contracts manager for a company that produced rocket fuel for the air force. I took my mug into the living room. I sat on the sofa facing my father's chair—his visualizing chair, his imagining chair, the chair that had helped him live six years when the doctor told him he had no more than six months.

I leaned forward into the steam from the mug. I half closed my eyes and squinted just a bit.

"Dad...So Donnie Couch has this train set..."

The End

ABOUT THE AUTHOR

TONY JORDAN GREW UP ON the Gulf Coast of Alabama and attended the University of the South (Sewanee), where he received a bachelor's degree in religion and theology. He flew long-range combat-rescue helicopters in Southeast Asia during and after the Vietnam War. He obtained a master's degree in political science from Auburn University and worked as a clandestine operations officer at the Central Intelligence Agency for over twenty-six years, rising into the senior ranks of the Clandestine Service. During his time with the CIA, he lived in Sri Lanka, India, Rome, London, and a number of "they shall remain nameless" locations in the Middle East and Africa. After leaving the CIA, Tony served as a senior vice president with a Boston-based high-tech firm. In 2013 he retired to write from a mountain hideaway in East Tennessee. He is a highly decorated intelligence officer and pilot as well as an award-winning author.

Made in the USA
Charleston, SC
18 October 2016